The Last Leaf

By *Devon Hoole*

Devon Hoole

DEDICATION

"We were promised sufferings. They were
part of the program. We were even told,
'Blessed are they that mourn,' and I accept it.
I've got nothing that I hadn't bargained for. Of
course it is different when the thing happens
to oneself, not to others, and in reality, not
imagination."

C.S. Lewis

In Loving Memory

Granny Phyl Mason

23 April 1931 – 16 October 2020

Foreword

The idea for the story came to me when I was on holiday with my dad (one of my all-time favourite trips). We were lying on the bank of a river and I was looking up into the branches of a tree. The wind was blowing and leaves continually fluttered off towards the ground. It made me wonder how many people have managed to watch the last leaf fall off a tree, and what a magical moment that would be. It spoke of a new season and a chance to begin again. This story was written with the intention to show a journey that the character embarks on and how new seasons can be painful and scary, but they are part of life, and cannot be avoided.

Devon Hoole

The Last Leaf

Making sure I was unseen, I listened quietly by the door as my parents whispered in the kitchen. My mother's voice clipped in fright, while my father spoke soothingly, despite the fear that held his throat. The day's light was disappearing, and I had just awoken from a nap, which meant I would have another sleepless night, but the silence that had hung in the house as I had awoken made my stomach clench. The quiet whispers from the kitchen were the only sounds that penetrated the silence. When I got close enough, I heard my mother speaking first.

"What do you mean Clay caught the last leaf? How could he have? I don't understand."

Understanding lit my mind. This was about Clay. My older brother was always up to some mischief and getting himself in trouble, which is why he was my hero. I wished that I were more like him; he was popular, funny, and could charm anyone. I, on the other hand were none of those things, but at least I had Clay around so I could live vicariously through him. I brought my thoughts back to what my mom had said, and I wondered what catching the last leaf meant. A story about a leaf tickled the back of my mind, but I couldn't identify where it came from. My father continued speaking, and I silently moved closer to hear better.

"Come on honey, you know the story of how the tree supposedly works. We've never even seen the last leaf fall off, but Clay had been watching that tree for months. He caught it and was taken."

"Taken where? Where did my boy go?"

"How am I supposed to know? I always thought it was a fairy-tale," the silence stretched out. I wondered if the conversation had ended, but suddenly he spoke again, "All that I know is that I saw him under the tree, and then the next moment he disappeared. I have searched everywhere for him, but there's no sign of him anywhere. You know that he became obsessed with that tree ever since…"

"Don't you dare speak of such things under this roof. I will hear none of it. Clay is fine, I'm sure he will walk back through the door any moment. He always liked to disappear for a while, but he would always come back. He has an adventurous soul."

By now I was close enough to see my parents standing side by side in the kitchen. All the men in the family looked the same, we all had sandy brown hair and green eyes, similar heights of about six foot. Although my dad's hair was showing tinges of grey, he still looked strong and sturdy. He was washing the dishes while my mom furiously dried them next to him. Mom's hands always needed to be busy when she's nervous. She was a lot shorter than the rest of us, but she made up every inch with her powerful personality.

He was shaking his head slowly, "Honey, you know this time it's different. You have heard the stories about the tree, and what happens when someone catches the last leaf that falls off. The earth shakes and everything goes quiet for a few seconds. That's exactly what happened earlier today!"

I heard a sob come from my mom as she looked out the window at the darkening evening. I could see the outline of four large trees dancing in the wind, "But maybe it was just a coincidence…"

He spoke firmly, "Clay had been under that tree, the earth shook, everything went quiet, and then he was gone." His voice softened again, "It was no coincidence, and now all we can know is what the story told us about what happens on the other side. I can't believe what I'm saying, but I see no other explanation."

Suddenly I realised what they were talking about and tried to remember parts of the story I had been told. I leaned in closer; I had never heard the full story of the last leaf. Whenever our uncle Telly had told the tale, our parents would silence him with a warning look. Whenever uncle Telly had looked after us, we would try to get the full story out of him. But even offering him a few too many drinks was never enough to loosen his tongue. I wondered if Clay had finally heard the full story… that would explain his renewed obsession with the tree.

I couldn't believe that he had caught it. Together they had tried for years, but had never gotten close before. Either all the leaves wouldn't fall off, or they would wake up one day and it was all bare. I wondered how he had been watching the tree without me realising it. Although, to be honest, I didn't notice much of what happened outside. Why hadn't Clay told me about it?

"We can't tell Lino just yet." My ears perked up at the sound of my name. "We need to search for Clay a bit longer before we tell Lino anything. You know how he gets when things are uncertain. I don't have the energy to deal with that now." A sob stopped her from talking, and her shoulders started shaking from her tears. I stifled a yelp of fright as I heard a plate smash to the ground.

My dad gently took her shoulders and began herding her out of the kitchen. I realised they were heading right for me! I quickly retreated and headed back up the stairs to my room as I heard my dad offering her a cup of tea. My mind was spinning from their conversation. My parents had told me Clay had gone camping with some friends and would be back in a few days. I hadn't given it a second thought as he was often going away with friends and had a busy social life. Just the thought of all those people made me tired, I walked into my room and flopped onto my bed.

How had he watched the tree without me knowing? Surely I would've seen him if he had been hanging around here? It hurt me that Clay hadn't told me about it, he usually tried to include me in all his outlandish plans. I never did them, but why leave me out now? And why did my mom think I couldn't handle uncertainty? I could stand against adversity. How could they keep something as important as this from me? It was true; I wasn't great in stressful situations, but that's still no reason to keep me in the dark.

I scrunched up my pillow as I rolled over and stared out the window. So, Clay had caught the leaf, or at least that's what my parents were believing, but knowing Clay, I wasn't so sure. This could be another one of his jokes which he hadn't thought through and has now gotten out of hand. He will probably come back home in a few days with a goofy grin on his face. My parents would go ballistic and shout at him, but everything will go back to normal afterwards.

I sighed as I looked out the window into the grim night, maybe I would be lucky and fall asleep, or else the night would be long. Thoughts of Clay left my mind as I struggled with my own inner problems. I needed a change, something that would push me and force me to challenge myself. What could that be, though? I tried to ignore the despair that bubbled up and instead focused on finding some sleep.

⁂

I awoke the next morning with a headache, and I sighed at the normalcy of it. I was told that it was because of the tension I held in my shoulders from worrying too much, and that I needed to worry less. That had been expert advice, I shall just turn it off, will I? Silly me for worrying when I could just stop. I took some aspirin and headed downstairs. I was nearing the end of my gap year, and I was still clueless what to do next. Deciding what to study felt like a huge life decision and I didn't understand how people could make it so easily.

I shouldn't be trusted to make a decision like that, this could determine the rest of my life and I'm meant to make the smart decision now. I wasn't capable of that. For example, instead of using this year to figure out my next plan, I had wasted it at home with movies and books. What responsible, life-changing-decision-making adult would do that? I can't remember the last time I hung out with any old school friends, they had all gone off to college and I had remained at home.

I enjoyed being alone, but I also know that this amount of isolation is not good for me. I had tried at the beginning of the year to meet up with friends, but they had been so busy and then when we met up, it seemed like we had nothing in common any longer. From then on, the longer I was alone, the more comfortable I became with it. And I always had Clay to bring home wild stories. I had my parents and Clay, what else could I need?

As I walked into the kitchen, I knew my parents had been talking about Clay again because my mom greeted me with an exceptionally high squeal, "Good morning Lino, how are you this morning?" I shrugged an okay and got some cereal. She continued in a more human tone, "So I invited your uncle Telly to come stay with us for a few days, he'll be arriving in a few minutes."

I paused mid-bite and looked at my dad in surprise. He just smiled and shrugged, happy that his brother was coming, but not willing to say it out loud. My mom had never invited uncle Telly over before. She always found him juvenile, and he had the natural skill of getting under her skin. I saw she was flushed as she bustled out the kitchen. Clay's disappearance must be more serious than I thought. Interesting, so they are taking this seriously, or at least they are desperate enough to go to uncle Telly for help.

After breakfast, I wandered out the back door into the garden. We had an expansive garden, but it was mostly made up of grass, and then four enormous trees that stood guard on the far perimeter. Many games and a lot of fun was had in this garden, Clay and I had played every game imaginable, usually led by Clay's imagination and his rules. But the most fun we had was in the Magi forest that started just beyond our trees. That wasn't the forest's official name, but we had always thought the forest was magical and so that's what it became known as.

I wandered over to the four trees and tried to recall any stories we had overheard about them. We were told that each of us had our own tree, and they were symbolic of our lives. Mine was the smallest. It looked weather beaten, but still stood strong. Three of the trees still had leaves, but Clay's branches were bare. Not a single leaf on the entire tree. That was odd. How had his come off so early? He must've knocked them off himself.

"Lino! Get back in this house immediately! Uncle Telly is here, and he needs help with his bags." I spun around in fright and paused at the fear on my mother's face. I started walking back to the house as she gestured frantically. A movement caught my eye, and I saw Leah, my next-door neighbour, staring at me through her window. I could only make out her black hair and dark eyes. Seeing her again brought me to a halt.

We had grown up together, but her stepmom had home-schooled her from matric, so we had drifted apart. Funny what two years could do to a friendship, and of course ignoring that person. I was ashamed to admit that the genuine reason for the break in friendship was that I had gotten caught up in my own life and started ignoring her. Apparently now she was studying online, but no one knew what subjects she was doing. I realised I was staring and lamely nodded a greeting in her direction and scampered back inside.

I broke into a grin as I saw uncle Telly. He always stood out in our house and looked misplaced. His messy grey hair and flamboyant clothing stood contrast to the order and bland colours in our house. He had always fascinated me; he had a freedom and easy-going nature that I envied. Actually, he was like Clay in many ways, both were charismatic and fun to be around, and both gave my mom a hard time. Uncle Telly enveloped me in a hug and gave me a few thumps on the back, "How are you doing youthful man? I hear that your brother has gone off on another adventure." My mom shot him a warning look, and he smiled innocently.

I grinned again and moved to take the bag from him, but he stopped me with a hand on my shoulder, "Thanks Lino, there's one in my car that you could fetch for me. This one I'll take myself." I saw books bulging in the bag and tried to read the titles, but uncle Telly shifted and blocked my view. I looked into his sharp eyes and saw the humour dancing in his gaze. He gave a little smirk and then headed upstairs with the bag. This was all getting strange, there was definitely something going on and I wanted to find out more about it. I needed to get my hand on some of those books, but for now, I turned around and got his bag from the car.

Throughout the rest of the day, I caught my uncle glancing outside at the trees. Every time we made eye contact, he would flash a quick smile and then look away. As I walked into any room it would quieten down, and they would all plaster smiles on their faces. He and my parents were constantly whispering to each other, and I even saw them eagerly leaning over a worn book. I headed back to my room and lay on the bed trying to figure this all out. I realised that I needed to get my uncle alone, he would be more willing to talk to me without my parents being there to quieten him. I was sure I could get him to tell me what was going on.

It must be about Clay and him supposedly catching the last leaf. I glanced out my window and saw Clay's tree, not a leaf was on it. I again wondered how he had done it. I tried to imagine what would happen if the legend were true. It said that the last leaf was a portal to an unknown world. What would it be like? Was it safe? What would he need to do before he could come back? What if he never returned, and the tree kept him forever?

I could feel my worry rising and quickly tried to distract myself. I wasn't sure if I believed any of this, but I still couldn't shake the tension in my stomach. I needed to think proactively, my dad had said the last time he had seen Clay he had been under the tree. Then he just disappeared, so if the last leaf is just a myth, then Clay was likely to be in the forest somewhere. I heard my mom call me down for supper, and as I headed down for dinner, I decided I would search the forest first thing tomorrow morning.

🌲 🌲 🌲

Early the next morning I yawned widely as I crept down the stairs and out the back door. The night had been long and sleepless, and I groaned as I felt the beginnings of another headache. Hopefully, some fresh air would help ease it. The ground was sprinkled with dew from the cool night, and I was glad I had worn my good boots. Too many times I had walked with soggy socks. Years of sneaking off into the forest had made me well aware of all the secrets to remaining comfortable, and now I was glad for it.

I felt eyes on my back as I ran along the grass and glanced around. I thought I saw the neighbour's curtain move, but I didn't slow down to check. Once I was past our four gigantic trees and into the forest, I let out a sigh of relief and headed deeper into the shading trees. I followed the well-worn path we had made over the years. Ankle high mist kept the ground covered, so I had to move carefully to avoid any hidden holes or branches. Instead of making everything spine-chilling, the mist made it more beautiful, and I sighed happily as I continued deeper into the Magi. I've always felt more comfortable out here, all by myself, than being around a room full of people. Following my room, this was one of my happy places.

Clay and I had spent many hours wandering around here and playing games we made up. We'd be hunters searching for our prey, sometimes we would be the ones hunted and we'd have to hide from the beast that was after us, or we would search for the lost princess. Clay was often the hero in the stories, but I was happy just to be part of the game. Clay was more of the hero-type anyway, and I liked to think of myself as the clever sidekick.

Concentrating on the task at hand, the first place I wanted to search was our old treehouse we built. We hadn't used it in a few years, ever since Clay had gone off to university, and without him, it never seemed as much fun. Although, calling it a tree house was a humorous stretch, as it was more of a few well-placed planks of wood that allowed us to sit up in the trees. We had thrown over a tarp that gave us cover from any rain that might fall, and this made it well hidden. Simplicity of design meant it blended in well with the surrounding greenery, and we placed it just above the lower branches, so we were out of view of anyone walking past. I climbed the thick trunk with ease and found our places empty. No sign of Clay.

I paused as I heard a crunching of leaves and twigs close by. I grinned and tried to remain as still as possible. If this was Clay, I was about to give him the biggest fright of his life. I peered through a gap in the branches to see how far he was from me. Disappointment arose as I saw Leah sneaking along as if looking for someone and not wanting to be seen. I watched as she paused and bit her nails; I felt annoyed that she was in our forest. It felt like an unwelcome intrusion into Clay and my world.

I made a rash childish decision and swung down into her path while screaming, hoping that I would at least scare her for the trespass. Clay and I had practiced this move many times in our defence against evil, but this time it didn't go so well. I over swung and my legs went out from under me. I landed flat on my back and gasped as my breath left my lungs. I remained on my back while I tried to gather my breath. I looked up as I heard giggling, Leah was attempting a concerned look, but it was not well composed.

She took a deep breath and asked, "Are you all right? Lino, what are you doing swinging out of trees like a mad person? You nearly scared me half to death." She hid her smile behind her hands.

I scrambled to my feet and tried to hide my embarrassment. Leah was a lot prettier than I remembered, she had long black hair and delicate features. Her cheeks were flushed from the exercise and it contrasted her pale skin nicely, but I could also see a darkness under her eyes that showed her tiredness. I briefly wondered if she also had trouble sleeping, but at the moment I needed to redeem myself, "I'm fine, what are you doing here?" I scrunched my eyes and tried to look menacing, "Were you following me?"

My directness seemed to catch her off guard, but she crossed her arms and replied, "Yes I was, I wanted to see where you were going. Are you looking for Clay?"

Now it was my turn to be thrown off, I hadn't expected that answer. My brain instantly froze, and my grasp on the use of words disappeared. My mouth opened and closed while I tried to come up with a witty response. This was why I disliked talking to girls - always felt like I was playing a chess game that I didn't understand the rules too, "I uh..." I tried to gather myself and puffed my chest out, "It's none of your business what I'm doing. I would like you to leave our forest."

This was the wrong thing to say, and Leah raised her eyebrows, "Your forest? This is a public space. I'm allowed to go anywhere I like."

Part of why I avoided her resurfaced and my dislike for her increased. Tired from not sleeping the night before and feeling annoyed by her presence, I just wanted this conversation to be over, "Okay." I stepped to the side, "Carry on then, enjoy the rest of your walk."

She just stared at me for a few moments and then turned around and stormed away. I felt guilty as I watched her striding away. Maybe I should apologize. The intent remained, but I watched her disappear. I felt terrible, but I continued my search for Clay. Leah didn't deserve that; I shouldn't have snapped at her. It was my fault I had fallen from the tree, but still, she had no right to follow me. Leah had sucked all the magic and excitement from the air after my encounter with her, and I half-heartedly searched the last remaining spots that I knew. Clay was nowhere.

I dragged my feet the whole way home and as I emerged from the tree line, my mom's worried face met me. She let out a yelp of relief and I heard her call out that I was back. There was no sign of Leah anywhere, and as I neared the back door, my mom gripped my arm tightly and led me back inside as if fearful I might leave again. Uncle Telly was sitting at the table dressed in a camo coloured jumpsuit and wore an orange cap that read

'Don't shoot'. Pretending not to see him, I sat down and asked my mom, "Have you seen uncle Telly this morning? And do you know that there is an orange cap floating in mid-air?"

My uncle guffawed and nearly choked on his coffee, while my mom looked at me and him in confusion. Uncle Telly slapped me on the shoulder, "Good one boy, so you understand my need for the cap." He leant closer to me, "People don't like it when you are invisible, they need to know that I mean no harm, and that I'm not something to shoot at."

I grinned at him, "So are you going hunting or something?"

"Nope." I expected him to say more, but he took another sip of coffee and remained silent.

I laughed, "Okay, glad that's settled then. So, here's a question for you, have you ever been shot at before?"

He nodded enthusiastically, "I have, although not in the normal sense. I was watching T.V when out of nowhere this…" My mom cut him off with a firm look. He just shrugged and headed to the lounge with a laugh.

I chuckled, and wondered what not being shot at in the normal sense meant, but then my mom turned her scowl on me and I fell silent, "Lino, your father and I are going out for a while. We will be back in a few hours. In the meantime, your uncle Telly is here, and he will look after you."

"Mom, you remember I'm not a child that needs a babysitter. To think of it, I don't think we've ever had a babysitter." I paused and then asked, "What's going on, anyway? Just tell me; I can handle it."

She hesitated, but then shook her head and put on an extra cheery smile, "I misspoke darling. Of course you don't need anyone to look after you. Uncle Telly is just here because he has nowhere else to be." A loud laugh came from the living room. We both smiled at each other as my dad came down the stairs. She kissed me on the forehead and headed for the door, "Oh, and don't listen to too many of uncle Telly's stories or they'll rot your brain."

I walked into the living room and dropped into a chair opposite my uncle. He was reading a book so worn that I couldn't make out any of the writing on the cover. I decided that this had to be my chance to try to finally get some answers out of him, "Uncle Telly? I was wondering…"

He cut me off, "Sorry boy, I can't give you the answer you want. They've sworn me to secrecy." He remained hidden behind his book, but I could see he was struggling to keep the story to himself. This was a rare opportunity for a captivated audience, and he knew it. It would eat him inside to keep silent.

I changed tact, "Actually I was wondering about next year, and what you think I should study?"

This got the reaction I desired, and he immediately lowered the book, "Well, now that's a significant question. I never finished school myself, and I wouldn't trust higher education with a ten-foot pole, but I'm sure there is something out there for you."

Encouraged that I got him talking, I said, "It's such a big decision, and I don't want to mess it up. If I pick the wrong thing, I could be miserable for the rest of my life." My anxiety was raising its head, but this was the first time I'd mentioned my fears, and it seemed to help a bit. Even though I wanted to talk about Clay, I realised that this was also something that had been on my mind.

My uncle looked at me, "That's a lot of pressure to carry in one decision." He paused as he got into a more comfortable story telling position, "Let me tell you a story. Did you know that I was married?"

I shook my head in surprise; I had always thought he didn't believe in marriage and would've had some crazy theory about signing a contract with another person. Uncle Telly continued, "It was a long time ago. We both were seventeen, she fell pregnant and so I dropped out of school and started working to support us. Unfortunately, we lost the baby." His eyes sheened with moisture; I had never seen such sadness in his eyes before. He continued with a crack in his voice, "We didn't know how to cope with the loss, and so we headed our separate ways. Now, this was a major life decision we made; it affected the rest of our lives. Do you think it ruined my life because of that decision?" He arched an eyebrow.

I quickly shook my head, "Of course not. To be honest, I'm actually jealous of the life you've led."

He chuckled, "My life is my own and you mustn't try to replicate someone else's story. Here's the hard truth about adult decisions: They have consequences and sometimes they have long-term effects, but if you don't make any decisions at all, it's a lot worse. You'll find yourself becoming miserable and bitter. You'll feel that life owes you something, and that'll only make things worse for you. One decision has hundreds of outcomes, trying to predict those outcomes will only stress you out. My advice to you is to just choose something. If it's the wrong decision, you'll be able to alter course and try something else. But Lino, you need to try. Don't hide away from the world - you have too much to offer."

I sat awkwardly as I digested what he had just said. This had gotten a lot heavier than I had imagined, and I had never heard him be serious for so long before. I shifted under his steady gaze and tried to change the subject before he gave me any harder truths. I suddenly remembered part of the story about the last leaf. I said, "Well, maybe I should take another year off before I decide. I could travel for a bit, do some backpacking somewhere, maybe a pilgrimage." I glanced up at him to see his reaction, and I immediately knew I had not been subtle enough.

Uncle Telly had an enormous grin on his face, "You sneaky rascal, I knew you knew! You are too smart not to be aware of what's going on." He leant back in the seat and watched me curiously, "So tell me what you know and your theory about it all, and then we can see where we go from there."

A breakthrough, I excitedly started talking, "I overheard mom and dad talking about Clay catching the last leaf. They said that the earthquake and the quietness that followed was what happens when someone catches the leaf. This is where things get foggy for me, and I can't remember the story except for a rough overview. My parents always stopped you short when you tried to tell us. All I remember is that the leaf transports you to an unknown world. A place where you have to go on a pilgrimage, and you face challenges along the way.

My theory is that you and my parents believe that he caught the leaf and now he's gone. That's why you have all these books and are whispering in corners… you are trying to figure out how to get him back. Although I'm convinced he's just hiding somewhere as a joke. I suspect Clay felt the earthquake and thought this would be the perfect opportunity to trick us all." I stopped and waited for my uncle's response.

He nodded slowly, "I promised your parents I wouldn't tell you what happened or what the story of the Last Leaf was about." He cleared his throat, "And you know I am a man of my word and so I can't tell you everything, but since you know about Clay, I feel I can confirm a few things for you." Again, he paused, and I felt the tension building, "You brother is not playing a joke on us. He caught the last leaf and has disappeared."

"Come on uncle Telly, you can't be serious. You can't believe that Clay has gone to a different world? To do what? Go on a pilgrimage? That's crazy, even for you." I felt annoyed by his eagerness to confirm a fairy-tale.

He remained serious though, "I know it's real because I have caught the last leaf myself." He paused for dramatic effect but then continued in a softer voice, "Right after we lost our baby, I was in a low place and spent a lot of time beneath those trees. I'd also heard of the stories about the last leaf, and then the next thing I know, I saw a golden leaf fall towards me. As soon as I caught it, I disappeared and re-appeared on a grassy hilltop." Grudgingly for both of us, he stopped himself, "I can't tell you more than that, but it's very real."

I was struggling to process what he had just said, "What do you mean you've been there! That's not possible." I waited for the laugh and a slap on the shoulder, but it didn't come. He only watched me silently. Slowly I realised that he was being serious. My mouth fell open, and I spluttered, "Well, now you have to tell me what happened! You can't leave me hanging like this." I couldn't believe what I was hearing, but the look on uncle Telly's face told me he believed it. The Last Leaf was real, and Clay had caught it. "But you made it back, so Clay will also be back soon. How long does it take?"

He shook his head, "Time is different, it could be a few moments, or he could never come back. I barely made it back myself. I had only been gone half a day before I was back, although I had spent an entire week in Paradis."

"Paradis? Is that what they call the place?" Another thought hit me, "So, it's really bad that Clay had been gone this long, something could be wrong?"

"Listen, Lino, I can't tell you anything more. I've said too much already. The last thing I will say is that you must not try to follow him. I know you will want to, but it's not worth it. You'll just have to take me at my word this time. We need you here. Your parents need you here, they will not cope if you go as well. We need to trust that Clay is fine and will be back soon." He stood up and patted me on the shoulder as he walked past. He left me alone with my thoughts.

🌲 🌲 🌲

Despite uncle Telly's warning, I became obsessed with the four trees, and I could think of nothing else. Whenever my mom let me out of her sight, I would slip outside and sit beneath the trees. One tree was bare already, Clay's tree, but the other three were continuing to drop their leaves. One of them, my smaller one, was losing leaves faster than the other, and this was the one I focused all my attention on. I kept the tree insight at all times and always sat by a window when I wasn't outside. I even moved my bed, so I had a better view of my tree.

I wasn't taking any chances and there was no way I was missing this opportunity.

The days stretched out and after a week there was still no sign of Clay, and my tree was not losing leaves fast enough for my liking. My parents were not coping well. The house had grown quieter every day, and even uncle Telly seemed to lose some of his energetic nature. They had sat me down yesterday and told me what they thought happened to Clay in a sombre tone. I already knew all they told me, and when I tried to ask questions, they wouldn't tell me anything new.

My frustration increased. I realised that they didn't know more than me, and uncle Telly, who knew the most, was not willing to talk of his experience. On top of everything, he had also left yesterday, and promised he would be back in a few days once he got more information. He said that he knew a guy who might tell them something new. I couldn't handle the unknown and just waiting around. I decided I needed to do something about this.

I awoke early the next morning and headed out to the tree. I couldn't see any difference, and no fresh leaves had fallen off for days now. My desperation welled, and I jumped up to the nearest branches and plucked off a few of the leaves. I scrunched the leaves in my hands and angrily tossed them aside. I waited for something to happen, for some penalty for touching the leaves. Nothing happened, and I laughed bitterly.

Of course nothing would happen. This was a tree like every other. Nothing special about it, and I had fooled myself into believing that it held the key to another world and that Clay was not missing but had just gone off on a fantastical journey. Suddenly I froze. Would the tree still work if I pulled off leaves? Even though I didn't fully believe it, I didn't want to do anything that might jeopardize the possibility.

Would this still work? I had sneaked a few glances of the books that uncle Telly had brought, and they had mentioned nothing about how the leaves came off, only that the person had to catch the last one. I couldn't believe that I still hoped for the impossible. A frenzy overtook me, and I couldn't stop myself, I began pulling off as many leaves as I could reach.

Once I couldn't reach anymore leaves, I tried to decide how to get the rest off. I would need to get up into the tree, but the trunk had no agreeable places for me to climb. As I was contemplating my next move, I heard a cough from behind me. I looked over and sighed as I saw Leah; she was watching me again. I tried to ignore her, but now that I knew she was there all I could think of was that she must've seen me jumping around like a crazy person.

I felt like I had to explain myself, "I'm trying to get rid of all the leaves, they are taking too long to fall off."

Leah smirked, and I realised how crazy I had just sounded. I was about to explain further but I asked, "Are you just going to sit there and watch me? Don't you have anything better to do?"

"And miss all the fun, no chance, I want to see if you can get them all off. I get it. If the tree isn't performing, then you need to help it along and make sure all the leaves come off before winter. Are you going to do the entire forest? A lot of these trees seem to be slacking off and will need your help."

I flushed in embarrassment and turned back to face the tree, it was looking rather barren but there were still tufts of leaves spread throughout, "Whatever, you won't understand."

"Are you trying to catch the last leaf? Will it work if you get rid of all the other leaves, isn't that cheating?"

I froze and turned towards her in amazement, "How do you know about that?"

She shrugged and began walking next to the small fence that separated our back gardens, "We had your mom over for tea and she told us." Leah leaned on the fence, "You don't believe it do you? It's a bit, well, off the wall." She gazed up at the tree and then back at me, her dark eyes making me feel foolish as I stood among ripped off leaves, "Well I guess you do."

I looked down at my feet, "Yeah well, my parents are a mess and I can think of nothing else to do. So," I spread my arms, "I am improvising."

Leah's laugh chimed in the quiet morning, and I couldn't help grinning back. She nodded towards the tree and turned back towards her house, "I would suggest using a ladder to get to the more tough spots and the stubborn places, or just cut off the branches. Try not to fall out this one."

I watched her leave and felt even more confused than ever before. Although, a ladder was not a terrible idea. It would solve my immediate problem. I got the ladder, and a sharp saw, and then propped it against the trunk. I climbed the tree and continued plucking the leaves; I broke off branches and sawed off a few. I nearly fell off a few times and stopped when I realised that going any higher would become dangerous.

Once back on the ground I looked at my handiwork. The tree looked barren except for two little patches that I could not get to. I had scattered leaves and branches all over the floor. It looked like the trees had fought and this one had come out as the definite loser. I was pleased with my work and wondered if it would still work now that I had sped up the process.

I went back to the house and packed myself some food and brought a chair outside. I was taking no risks; this was my shot, and I would not miss it. My parents were rarely leaving their room anymore, so it was easier for me to move around. Hopefully, the last few leaves would fall off before uncle Telly came back. He definitely seemed to still be monitoring me and seemed to know what I was up too. There was also a worried look in his eyes whenever he looked at me that I didn't understand.

The day passed extremely slowly as I sat beneath the tree, and I dozed off often. I heard Leah's backdoor open a few times during the day, but I refused to look or see if she was there. I didn't want to see her smirking face telling me that this was a futile idea; I was fully committed now, and I didn't want to doubt myself. A strange wind started blowing as the sun disappeared and a few more leaves fell off. There were only a handful left. I quickly rushed back inside to restock my snacks, grab a torch, and get a blanket. I decided I would spend the night under the tree, seeing as it was too risky to sleep tonight. Luckily, I usually struggled to sleep anyway, so this would be no problem and I felt wide awake.

During the next few hours, the wind continued to blow, and more leaves came tumbling down. I kept checking with my torch and was shocked when I saw three leaves left. I walked around and looked at every part of the tree, but I was certain these were the last three. I moved my chair under the spot and continued to wait. If this swirling wind continued, it would be difficult to catch the leaf as it was carrying them in different directions. I continued to doze off as the night lengthened and I would wake up with a fright, quickly switching on the torch. Still three left.

I awoke suddenly and fumbled for my light but realised I didn't need it as there was a dim glow beginning to illuminate the sky. My breath quickened as I realised that only one leaf was left, I must've missed the other two coming off. As I was wondering what had awakened me so suddenly, I realised that the wind had disappeared. I looked at the surrounding trees and there wasn't a branch moving. Everything was still. The next thing I noticed was the lack of noise. There were no birds or insects making their morning greetings.

I heard a loud crack, and then multiple things happened at once. Out of the corner of my eye I saw Leah jump the fence and start running towards me, our back door burst open and my uncle Telly was shouting for me to run from the tree, and then I turned my head upwards and saw the last leaf falling towards me. The leaf had turned golden and fell in slow motion; I reached out my hands as it twirled closer. The golden leaf reflected my face, and I saw the desire in my eyes, and then it flipped over, and I saw a wide-open field. Constantly shifting between my face and the field, it continued falling towards me.

As my hand was about to snatch the leaf out of the air, I felt a hand grasp my shoulder. I caught the leaf, my world exploded, and everything went dark.

Paradis

I lay on my back staring up at a blue sky, wondering what had just happened. I heard a groan next to me and looked over - to my shock; it was Leah. She was also lying flattened on her back. I propped myself up and froze as I realised we were no longer in my backyard. A wide-open field that sprawled off into the distance replaced tall trees and forest. We were on a small hill that gently sloped downwards in every direction. I marvelled at the greenness of the grass as I stood up.

This was no ordinary place. Even the air felt lighter and a flowery scent filled my senses. I looked around but couldn't see any flowers nearby and realised it must be the natural smell. A light breeze came across the hill-top, but other than that, the weather was perfect. I looked farther and realised that four paths led from our position into different directions running away from us.

I followed one with my eyes and thought I saw a tiny village at the end, with a vast mountain-range in the distance. I turned and followed another one. It also led to a small village, but a forest backdropped this one. Another village was on the shore of a vast body of water, and the last path led to another village that had a desert behind it. Or at least that's what I thought it looked like. It definitely looked barren and not a place you wanted to find yourself stranded in.

I heard Leah gasp next to me and we both stared at each other in shock. She steadied herself by holding my arm as her eyes searched our new surroundings, "It's real, I can't believe it. You were right."

Her touch made me freeze, and with the wonder of our unfamiliar environment, all I managed was to grunt my agreement. The moment stretched on and I felt uncomfortable by her closeness, so I took a step away from her and walked in a small circle while I gazed intently at everything. Four villages with very different settings behind them - I didn't understand how that was possible. I was still trying to process everything as Leah's question came, "What do we do now?"

I looked at her, and for the first time realised she was actually here. Somehow, she had come with me. I asked, "How did you get here? I was the one who caught the leaf. You shouldn't have been able to come here without your own leaf."

She bit her nail, "Well, I had been watching you the entire night and then when I recognised the change in weather, I knew something was about to happen, so I jumped the fence and held on to you as you caught the leaf." She looked apologetically at me, "The weather changed the same way before Clay disappeared."

What she said took a few moments to sink in. My voice fell silent, "How do you know that the weather changed before Clay disappeared? I remember the earthquake, but nothing about everything going quiet."

Leah looked away, and I saw tears form in her eyes, "I saw him disappear. I had been outside watching him obsess over the tree, just like you did, and he told me what his plan was. I didn't believe him, but it intrigued me to see what would happen. Next thing I know, he catches it..."

She looked at me pleadingly, "… and then everything was just crazy from there. I was too scared to tell anyone what I saw, but then I realised you were trying the same thing, so I began watching you. When you began pulling the leaves off and said you thought there was a loophole, I realised that maybe if I held on to you, then I wouldn't need to catch the leaf myself." She had been speaking faster as she saw the look in my eyes. She ended quietly, "I guess it worked."

My anger made me shake. She had known where Clay had gone all along. A slight part of me was also jealous that she had been watching Clay, "You saw him disappear, and you didn't tell me! How selfish of you to keep that to yourself. We thought he had just left." The build-up of emotion and the shock of the last week overcame me and made my voice crack. I turned away from Leah as tears filled my eyes. There was no way I would let her see me cry. I looked over at the desert area and tried to push down my emotions. It embarrassed me that this was happening, I was never this emotional.

"Lino."

I ignored her and continued looking in the opposite direction, trying to calm myself down. She had known all along that Clay had disappeared. Now it made sense why she kept watching me and followed me into the forest. Why had Clay told her about his idea, and not me? Her voice came again, more urgent this time, "Lino!"

I turned around, ready to shout again, but when I saw what she was looking at my tongue fell limp in my mouth. There was a man sitting cross-legged on the grass, watching us. He was dressed in a blue suit and strangely, with sandals, also blue. Leah gasped, and I followed her eye-line. Another man sat in a green suit, with green sandals. I turned further and two other men casually rested on the ground, one with a black suit and the other with a camel colour, both with matching sandals.

I bumped into someone and gave a yelp, quickly turning to see that it was Leah, and she was equally frightened. We remained close as we watched the mystery men. I realised they were all the same. Except for the colour of the suits and sandals, they had the same black hair, and their faces were identical, not a strand of hair different.

As I looked at each man, they smiled but said nothing. Their lack of movement and friendly smile gave me some courage, so I turned to the man in blue. The colour seemed more inviting than the others. I asked, "Who are you? What do you want?"

The man smiled again and nodded, "We are here to welcome you to Paradis." Leah and I clutched each other as all four men spoke in unison, "Welcome!"

The man in the blue suit continued, "The Prince has sent us here to give you a choice."

Green suit picked up the narrative, and we turned to him, "This rarely happens, so you are being offered a gift. The Prince is generous in all of his ways." A mumble of agreement came from the four men.

Black suit continued, "We are here to offer you the opportunity to go home. The Prince knows how you got here and why you did it, so he is offering you the chance to return to your own world. If you continue, the Prince has allowed you to travel together, instead of doing the journey alone as you normally would be expected to. The Prince is kind to those who need it." The mumble of agreement came again.

We had nearly turned a full circle as the man in the camel suit spoke. He was the only one who didn't smile, "But know this: If you continue, you will need to reach the Prince's city. There is no going back once you embark on the journey. The only way is to make it to the Prince, and then he will decide whether to grant you passage back home. Yet, there is no guarantee that your journey to him will be successful."

Blue suit finished, "The choice is yours; do you wish to continue or return home?"

I looked at Leah, her mouth hung open and she just shrugged. I asked the men, "Do you know what has happened to my brother Clay? He came here about a week ago. He looks similar to me, same height, brown hair. Have you seen him?"

The man in the blue suit shook his head, "We may not speak about other travellers, all he permits us to speak to you about is your decision. If you stay, you will have to figure out the rest yourself, as others have done before you."

"So, others have done this journey before… How many makes it back home?"

All the men just stared at us and remained silent. I looked back at Leah, "So what do you think? What do you want to do?"

She was biting her nail again, "I'm not sure. It all sounded a lot more fun when it was just a fairy-tale. Now that I'm here it doesn't seem as good of an idea. Maybe we should go back? Clay could have made it back already."

Clay would have definitely chosen to continue the journey; he wouldn't have turned back. I looked at each man again and realised that their suit colour matched the surroundings behind the towns. Each one sat next to the path that led to the villages. I knew which one Clay would have chosen. Leah's answer had helped me make my decision. I looked the man in the blue suit straight in the eyes, "Leah will go home, and I will continue."

"Wait! No, if you're staying then I am as well."

I turned angrily on her, "Don't be foolish, you just said you wanted to go home. Clay is my brother and I will find him, while you must go back home and worry about your own family."

She crossed her arms stubbornly, "I don't have to do anything, and if I want to come with, then that's what I will do."

"Hey, wait!" I shouted to the men who had suddenly risen and were walking away, "Where are you going? Leah needs to go back home."

The man in the camel coloured suit spoke over his shoulder, "You both have made your decision, good luck with your journey to the Prince. Oh, and one more thing, make sure you stay on the path and not stray far from it. Remain on this hill tonight, and then tomorrow you may begin." With that, the men faded from our view.

I looked at Leah and shook my head, "Why wouldn't you go? That was your chance to go home safely. Who knows what will happen now? You might never see your parents again!" I searched her eyes to see what she was thinking, "I don't get it. Does Clay mean this much to you?"

Leah blushed bright red, "No, it's not that. I just… Do you smell that?" She turned around and gasped, "Lino, look. Where did these tents come from?"

It amazed me what I was seeing. Someone had set two plain small tents up, and a small fire with a pot was blazing between them. I walked closer and saw something bubbling in the pot. It smelt delicious. It seemed to be some type of vegetable broth. I peered into the tents and found cushions and sleeping bags. There was no sign of anyone.

Leah had already taken a seat on a log beside the fire and was stirring the soup, "This is weird, right? This was definitely not here a few moments ago. Just like the men, they seem to have appeared out of thin air."

This was all too much for me. Nothing was making sense, and impossible things were already happening. I paused and wondered if I could fly. Leah was looking at me and I decided I would try later when she wasn't around to see. My stomach rumbled as another waft of the soup reached me, but I remained standing, "I'm not sure we should eat that, we don't know where it came from. What if someone did something to it?"

"Don't be ridiculous," Leah took out a small spoonful and took a sip, "This is fantastic! Lino, relax and take a seat."

I grumpily took a seat and watched the fire flicker. I looked around as another oddity struck me, "It's getting dark already. When we left home, the sun was just coming up, so we've lost an entire day by coming here, it felt immediate to me, but I guess it must've taken a lot longer."

Leah was putting some soup in a wooden bowl and then handed it to me. I was suspicious, but my hunger won out and I started eating. I rarely liked soup, but this was different; all the flavours worked perfectly together, and I even refilled my bowl twice more. We sat in silence while we ate, and despite being in an unknown place and having better things to worry about, I couldn't help but think about Clay and Leah.

It made sense that she would be interested in him. He is like the upgraded version of myself. All charisma and charm, and a sense of danger surrounded him that girls seemed to love. I wouldn't have thought Leah would be interested in him. It had always come across that his presence annoyed her. Considering my lack of understanding in that department, I would imagine that was a clear sign she liked him. As I stared at the fire, I wondered how Clay was doing and where he was. He was probably having the time of his life here, just enjoying every moment and making friends everywhere he went.

And how would I fare in Paradis? I had never gone on an adventure without Clay and, without fail, he had always been around to help me out of situations. Not having him around left me feeling exposed. I glanced over at Leah and she was biting her nails. At least it was easy to tell when she was nervous. Seeing her nerves helped calm me down a bit. I realised I had been harsh with her, and it was nice to have someone else around.

I wanted to make amends, but the words wouldn't come out. When I cleared my throat, my mistake became apparent as she looked at me expectantly, I said the first thing that came to my mind, "So who do you think this Prince is? It was weird how they spoke about him, especially when they all spoke in unison."

Leah looked thoughtful, "I was wondering the same thing, the men in suits said we had to get to him, and he was our only way out of here." She shrugged, "I guess we will find out more along the way. So, our immediate decision is which path we will take, we have four options and who knows which one will take us to him. If we pick the wrong one, it could head us in the complete opposite direction that we need to go."

I tried to think which path Clay would have taken. He wouldn't have headed to the desert or sea, but he would be keen to head to the forest or the mountain range. Clay had always loved the mountains, but we rarely had an opportunity to explore some, so that could be an understandable reason for him to head that way. We were both familiar with the forest, so maybe he would not feel interested enough to go there. I know I would pick the forest, but I had this feeling that Clay would have picked the mountains.

"You know, if we will do this together, it would help if you spoke to me more. I never know what you are thinking, and you often seem lost in your own world." Leah was watching me with those dark eyes again, I shrunk a little under her gaze. The focused attention was making me uncomfortable; I wasn't used to someone asking me for my opinion. This is when I really wished Clay was with me. He would have done enough talking for the both of us.

My discomfort made me stand up and sheepishly say, "I'm feeling tired, it's been a crazy day, so I'm going to head to bed." I saw the look of hurt flash across Leah's face, but I quickly slinked into my tent and avoided any further conversation. As I lay in my tent, I groaned at my cowardice, and kept replaying the scene over in my head. I heard Leah get into her tent and settle down. She called out my name quietly, but I remained silent. I wasn't in the mood to speak anymore. I'll try to make it up to her tomorrow.

Although I had so many thoughts running through my mind, I fell asleep quickly and dreamt many strange dreams. Most of them involved Clay calling out for my help while I remained just out of reach. Sometimes I would call him to help me, but he never heard and would continue scaling rocks with incredible speed. The roots of trees came alive, and I screamed as I saw them wrapping around Leah's legs and begin pulling her deeper into the forest. As she was being pulled away, Clay stood off to the side, motioning for me to follow him.

To my disgust, I followed Clay and left Leah to fend for herself. Then Clay and Leah were walking together, while something trapped me up in a tall tree, watching them go past. The four men in suits began chanting the Prince's name, and they forced me to watch Clay kneel before the Prince's empty throne.

I awoke from a dream where a large golden door had opened and the figure of a man had walked in the room to meet Clay. My heart was pounding as I lay in my tent, and I tried to remind myself they were only dreams. I quietly climbed out the tent and saw the beginnings of light. I paused as I searched the sky… there was no sun. I desperately searched, but the light was just coming by itself. By now I was accepting whatever happened, trying to figure it out just gave me a headache. I didn't have a headache this morning. That was a wonderful surprise.

I took a deep breath to calm myself and again enjoyed the smell of flowers in the air. A strange relief washed over me as I realized nothing new had magically appeared while we slept, and everything was still the same. The early morning was already pleasant, and I knew it would get warm today. I was keen to get started and begin our journey, the earlier the better. I was wondering how long Leah would still sleep, but at that moment she emerged from her tent with an enormous yawn.

I stifled a smile as I saw her hair going in all directions, I asked, "Morning, did you sleep well?"

She stretched as she nodded, "That was amazing, a few weird dreams, but other than that, it was the best sleep I've had in a long time."

"Yeah, I can see that," I hid my smile by turning away and tried to get my face under control. I turned back and found Leah furiously smoothing out her hair. I asked, "Did you notice a sun yesterday, because I can't find it?"

She continued irately flattening her hair, "Of course I saw it. It's rising from the..." She searched the sky and looked at me in shock, "There's no sun! Where's the light coming from?"

I shrugged as if it didn't bother me and I had already moved on to bigger issues, "Maybe when we get to the village, we can ask someone. I see we've got no left-over soup, so if we want breakfast we'd better start along a path."

Leah started chewing a nail as she asked, "Have you decided on a path? I was thinking maybe the forest would be a fitting place to start, as we are both familiar with that, but I guess any path could be the right choice?"

I glanced at each village again, but felt more certain this morning of which to choose, "I think Clay would have gone to the mountains, I feel he would have enjoyed a different scenery from what he's used to." Having said it aloud, it felt right, I knew that Clay went to the mountains.

Leah nodded in agreement, "Let's do it, I think we should leave the tents though. It doesn't look like we will carry them with us, they will be too heavy. We will just have to hope we can find somewhere along the way."

Worried that the decision had been mine to make, and now we were heading down a path I had chosen, my confidence wobbled. Leah was looking at me expectantly, and I tried to hide my fear. This is when I needed Clay. He would know what to do. Instead, I said, "Right, we might as well be off then." One last look at our temporary camp and then we began our trek into the unknown.

Lino and The Giant

The path that led away from the hilltop was rocky and the further along they went, it filled with sharp pebbles, while either side of them was still the soft green grass. Bigger rock shapes appeared to either side of them, and I guessed we should expect this as nearing a mountain generally became rockier. We had been walking for close to two hours, and my feet ached from every step on this rocky path. Somehow my boots were not helping at all.

Twenty minutes ago, Leah had hopped off the path and was walking on the soft green grass. She had told me to do it, but I refused, "Don't you remember we were told to stay on the path and not stray from it, I know you don't listen to anyone, but I will follow the rules they gave us."

Leah had groaned in pleasure as she took off her shoes and moved her feet on the soft grass, "I'm not straying from the path, I'm walking right next to it. I don't see why we have to torture our feet when there is a perfectly suitable alternative."

I secretly admired her carefree spirit. It reminded me of Clay, but at the same time the rebellious act got under my skin. They gave us rules for a reason, and I didn't want to break them. Why didn't she understand that? Especially when four men in suits magically appear out of the air, I assumed it would be obvious to listen to them. I just wanted to shout at her and tell her to get on the path, but I knew that wouldn't work, so instead I just remained quietly seething.

The pain from my feet was also making me irritable, so I continued wincing with every step, but refused to get off the path. I had to prove to Leah that this was the right way to do things, and not every rule had a loophole. There is nothing wrong with following the rules. I realised that Clay was the same, he would always have to push back on everything. Our parents told us to do something and he would have ten questions and then still find an unorthodox way to do it.

The annoying thing was that sometimes it worked, other times it backfired, but somehow, he always got away with it. He often teased me for following the rules, but I never understood the need to break them. They are there to make things easier, not to constrict you. I felt a lot of freedom within rules; they were my guide in life.

I glanced at Leah as she walked happily close by. The sight of her comfort made me even more angry. The distraction caused me to step on an especially sharp stone that seemed to make my boots paper thin. I yelped in pain, but quickly hid it with a cough and stubbornly continued limping along. Something was definitely off; my boots should've easily protected my feet.

"Everything all right?" I heard the laugh in her voice. I angrily waved her away and tried to walk faster, but it just made me look like I was walking on hot coals trying to avoid burning feet. I heard Leah's laugh behind me. I tried to focus on where I was stepping. If I looked for flatter stones, then it became more bearable. I heard Leah call my name, but I pretended not to hear her and continued walking. My name came again, but more urgent this time.

"Lino!"

I swung around to see Leah waving her arms and trying to pull her feet from the ground. I thought she was making fun of me for the way I had just been walking, so I turned and continued away.

Her tone was pleading, "Lino, I'm stuck. I can't move my feet, they seemed to have gotten glued to the grass."

I paused and then looked at her with a smug grin on my face, "Are you serious?" I laughed as I walked back along the rocky path to stand in line with her, "Why don't you just take off your shoes?"

Her face was furious, "Don't laugh, this is serious. I can't move!" She undid her shoes and stepped towards me, but her bare feet immediately fastened to the ground and she tumbled over. She screamed as her hands also glued to the ground, she yelled at me, "Lino, come help me! And stop laughing!"

Seeing her struggling on all fours was too funny for me, and it doubled me over laughing. I tried to control myself, "What do you want me to do? I don't want to get stuck as well. Maybe I should try to find someone to help you?" I made as if I were about to walk away.

Her head snapped up as she glared at me, "Don't you dare leave me here alone like this!" Her voice cracked, "Please don't leave me."

I sighed and tried to hide the satisfaction I felt. It felt good when I was right. I composed my voice and said, "I won't go anywhere, don't worry." For the first time, I thought of what I could do to help her out of this sticky situation, I smiled as I reminded myself to use that line on Leah later. I bent down to look at the grass. It looked no different from normal. I carefully plucked a single strand of grass and found that it also stuck to me. I couldn't get it off my fingertips, it seemed to become one with my skin. Out of desperation, I rubbed it on the rocky path. The grass fell off immediately.

"The path makes the grass fall off!" I shouted in triumph to Leah. However, another problem immediately presented itself, Leah was about five steps away from the path. I said with a smile, "I could just throw some rocks at you, maybe that would work?"

"Don't you dare! I don't want rocks thrown at me." She struggled extra hard against the grass, as if I were about to pelt her with rocks at any moment.

It tempted me, but I refrained. I looked up the path and saw that the rocks further along were getting bigger. I began walking towards them.

"Where are you going?" I could hear the fear in her voice.

"I see bigger stones up ahead. I will go fetch them and then hopefully create a little path to you. I'll be right back." I quickly hobbled to the larger stones and began gathering the flattest ones I could find. I got back to Leah and lay the first stone on the grass. Tentatively I put my hand on it to see if it would stick, but it remained a normal rock, no stickiness. I nodded to myself happily. I would just need ones that were big enough for my feet and so continued going back and forth until I had all the stones I needed. Hopping stone to stone to Leah, I got to her and couldn't help but say, "Thanks for staying put while I got to you."

Leah half laughed, half sobbed, "Stop it! What are you going to do now?"

I took the stone I was carrying and moved it towards her hand, "I guess I'm just going to get this under your hand." As soon as the stone touched her hand, her skin began coming free from the grass. We both whooped with joy.

I continued until both hands and feet were perched on stones, I helped her up and we hopped back to the path. As soon as we were back on the path, I felt Leah's body crash into mine and she buried her face in my neck as she clung to me. Happily, I held her for a few seconds but then extracted myself. My smugness was shining through, I was right about staying on the path and I had saved her, "Well, I guess I was right."

Annoyance immediately replaced her gratefulness, "You're such an ass! Why do you have to throw that in my face?" Tears filled her eyes, and she dropped to the floor with her head in her hands.

Stunned, I wondered what had just happened. I awkwardly stood by while she cried, and so, wanting to get away, I quickly hopped along the stones to get her shoes back from the grass. When I got back, Leah was sitting quietly looking away in the distance. I gave her the shoes and said, "I'm sorry, I shouldn't have said that. I'm just glad you are okay."

She sniffled while she took the shoes, "Thanks." She braved a wobbly smile, "It's just that all this is overwhelming, and I already feel guilty about not telling you about Clay. I'm never normally this emotional. It must be something in the air." She wiped her eyes, "I guess you were right about the path though."

I remembered my own teary experience and wondered if she was right. Suddenly I didn't feel like breathing the sweet air anymore. We looked at each other and laughed awkwardly. She remained seated, and I stood nearby pretending to look into the distance. After a few moments, Leah put on her shoes and then got back to her feet. I tentatively smiled at her and said, "Ready to continue?" She nodded and so we began walking slowly again. After a few moments, I couldn't help but say over my shoulder, "Glad we are out of that sticky situation."

The next thing I felt was a sharp pain in the back of my head, and I glanced a small rock hit the floor. I spun to Leah in shock as I held the back of my head, "What was that for?"

Leah spoke with all fake innocence, "What happened? I did nothing."

A smile broke onto our faces and we both laughed. Leah walked ahead of me and said, "Come on, let's get off this terrible path."

♣ ♣ ♣

We walked for another fifteen minutes, all the while the rocks got bigger and the grass disappeared until we only saw mountain all around us. Boulders rose to our side and blocked out the world. With no option but forward, we continued. Even the pebbled path was now a well-worn route that was a tremendous relief to my feet. Our steps echoed off the stone walls as we walked in silence. We turned a corner and found the man in the black suit perched on a boulder that looked like a throne. He sat in front of a solid wall; I could see no way through. I groaned at the thought of turning back and having to walk back over that dreaded path.

"Welcome Lino and Leah. I am thrilled you picked my path; this is by far the most beautiful of the villages. Before I allow you to enter, I have some questions." He paused as his eyes searched us, "How was the journey here?"

Leah and I looked at each other in surprise, I know I was expecting some riddle, not a question about how the journey had been. I answered, "It was fine, I guess. The rocky path was terrible on my feet, and we ran into a bit of a problem along the way, but other than that it wasn't so bad." Leah shot me a look of warning as if to tell me not to mention what had happened. I shrugged, not thinking about why I shouldn't mention it.

The man turned his gaze to Leah, "And you?"

I realised how terrible a liar Leah was, for when she responded, she had guilt written all over her face, "It was good, no problems really." Even her voice fell more silent as she spoke.

The man remained statuesque and continued to gaze at Leah. She shifted uncomfortably and looked at her feet. The man asked, "How are your feet?"

Leah's shoulders fell, and she looked up to him in desperation, "I thought it would be fine. I was walking right next to the path; it made little sense to torture our feet like that. I'm sorry I didn't listen, I didn't know…"

"You didn't know there would be consequences. I'm disappointed you broke the first rule so quickly, with a bit of discomfort, and you gladly disregarded our warning. And you," He turned his gaze to me, "You were doing so well until you also left the path. I was very disappointed when I saw that, very disappointed."

My face turned red with disbelief, "I only left the path to help Leah when she got stuck. I was helping her. Surely that's fine. I stayed on the path even when she asked me to join."

"Oh, thanks for selling me out Lino, that's just great." Leah folded her arms angrily.

"I told you not to leave the path!" I roared, the earlier anger returning, "Now I'm being blamed for helping you." I turned pleadingly to the man. His black suit seemed to blend in with the black wall behind him, and it felt like I was speaking to an immovable force, I begged, "We didn't mean to, it was an accident. We won't do it again. I was only off for a bit."

The man sadly shook his head, "If a rule is broken many times, or only broken once, the law has still been broken. In my eyes you are both guilty of an equal violation, and if it were up to me, I would leave you here to wander the mountains for the rest of your lives." He paused and took a deep breath, "But it isn't up to me." He sighed, "The Prince is merciful, and he has given you another chance." The stone walls seemed to murmur approval of the Prince, and then a deathly quiet fell again.

Leah and I both let out our breath in relief. We remained silent, too afraid to say anything else. For a moment, I had wondered if my chances of finding Clay were already over. Left to wander these mountains forever… now that wasn't a pleasant thought.

The man's black eyes watched us as if he were trying to decide what to do next. I couldn't help but notice him flexing and relaxing his toes in his sandals. I still didn't understand why they wore sandals with such a fancy suit. It made no sense.

The man spoke, and it brought me out of my sandal contemplation, "You may enter, but remember this. You may take nothing you find in this village. There are many treasures within, but if you take any on your journey, it will surely be your end. Not even the Prince will save you from that." He gestured for us to walk towards the wall.

We both looked at each other in confusion but obeyed and moved forward. As I got closer, I noticed a hidden crack in the rock wall that only revealed itself once you were a few feet away. It was dark, but I took a deep breath and took the step inside. I couldn't see anything, and I felt Leah bump into me and take hold of my arm. I tentatively took a few steps forward.

Nothing stopped me. That was an excellent sign. I made out a faint glow in the distance and moved towards it. The closer we got, the more easily we could walk. We got to the exit and walked into the light; it took our eyes a few moments to adjust to the brightness that assaulted our eyes.

The first thing that was blatantly obvious was everything was made of stone. The village seemed to have grown out of the rocky backdrop. Next was the abundance of precious stones that skilfully decorated everything, Leah whispered about diamonds and rubies, and the colours of the stones seemed to be endless.

The grim stone houses were littered with glittering adornments that gave this fortified village an air of royalty. Jasper, onyx and emerald stones were carefully lined around doors and windows. They even distinguished the floor we walked on with carefully designed artwork, all made of sardonyx, diamonds and more. I saw symbols I didn't understand sprawling across the floor, and some animals I'd never seen either. I shivered at the look of some of them and hoped we would never meet them.

"Clay! Let's go and…" A youthful man with ebony hair ran up to me, but stopped as he got a closer look. He frowned in confusion, and then fear flashed across his face. His appearance spoke of the hardness of the environment and he looked made of rock himself, yet all his clothes were lined with precious stones, and there was a large purple pendant that hung around his neck. Broad shoulders and a firm jaw belied his youthful face, he looked like someone had skilfully carved him out of stone.

He reddened slightly and turned to leave. He stammered as he tried to sneak away, "Sorry, I thought you were someone else."

I moved towards him, "Wait, do you know Clay? He's my brother, I've come looking for him. Could you please tell me where he is?"

The young Hercules look-a-like ignored me and rushed away. He was soon out of sight. I looked at Leah, "He knows Clay, he must be nearby." I couldn't help but break into a smile at our fortune. We started walking and followed a curved line of glittering rubies that led us through the centre of the stone village. We walked into a large open area that I guessed was the village square, and we found people clearing away merchant stores and decorations that were hanging everywhere. A parade of some sort must have happened recently.

A colossal statue stood in the centre of the square with writing beneath it. I made out the writing to say, 'The Prince'. I moved to get a closer look. This would be my first viewing of the Prince and I was keen to see what he would look like. The closer I got, the less of a man he appeared to be, there were so many precious stones decorating him, that I couldn't see what he looked like. It was definitely a figure of a man, but beyond that, it was all about the stones.

A sizeable man walked up to me and clapped me on the shoulder, "Beautiful, isn't it? Still considering leaving us?" He looked at me and gave a small start, but quickly recovered. He stuck his hand out to me, "Welcome to Bijou! I'm Ruben, the leader of this humble village."

The man had a crushing handshake and I could feel the callouses on his hand. His forearms were the size of my legs and his barrel chest spoke of his strength. He had long black hair that he had tied back, and a red pendant hung around his neck. Leah and I introduced ourselves and explained that we were looking for Clay. I asked him if he knew where Clay could be.

Ruben smiled, despite his large intimidating appearance. His smile was warm and friendly. He ignored my question and rather asked his own, "Has someone given you a tour yet? It would honour me to show you around and take you to go get your collier."

Leah and I looked at each other in confusion, she asked, "What's a collier?"

"Ah," Pleasure lit his eyes, and he reached for a pendant that hung around his thick neck, "This, my dear friends, is a collier. Everyone who stays in Bijou receives one of these. The choice of colour and stone is up to you, and it's yours to keep." The large man became lost to us as he gazed lovingly at his red stone. He seemed to remember us and laughed, "My apologies, I got lost in the beauty of my gift. The Prince is generous." The village rumbled assent of the Prince's generosity, but Ruben didn't seem to notice. "All right, let's begin."

From the square, we took a beautiful road filled with more stone's, and Ruben enjoyed showing us all the unique treasures and majestic homes that they had made. We walked past men and women working with stone, all of them large and muscular, but Ruben didn't introduce us to any of them, and none of them even glanced up at us as we walked past. Although everything was beautiful, something felt off about the place. I couldn't work out what it was, though. I wondered why no one greeted us or acknowledged our presence. I felt out of place in my simple clothes, while surrounded by such beauty.

Leah asked, "Where do you get all these beautiful stones from? I've seen nothing like it."

"And you never will see anything like it anywhere else, my dear. We're the only village who've been entrusted with this much riches. Our mountains are full of precious stones, and we mine them. Everyone that lives in Bijou is rich beyond measure." He grinned as he showed all the wealth we had walked past. "And now," he led us to a building with marble pillars and a gold encrusted door. We walked in and were met with stones of every colour that hung from the walls. "You may pick one each. Whichever catches your eye, you may take as your own."

I stood dazed, "What do you mean we may take one? We don't have any money."

Ruben laughed, "There's no cost, my young friend. This is a gift from us to you. We give every traveller that comes through here a collier."

Leah was already searching the wall. I hesitated a moment longer before I snapped out of my concern and eagerly went on my search. I knew nothing about stones and their value, so I went on colour alone, and also how it made me feel. I was shocked to find that certain stones made me feel differently. Some made my insides warm, while others made my skin itch. Each stone gave me a distinct feeling.

I stopped in front of a blue stone that pulled me in. Immediately, I picked it up and felt peace course through my body. I got lost in the stone's beauty, and only Ruben's firm hand on my shoulder broke my gaze from it. I looked up at him with a goofy, dazed grin on my face. He led me back to Leah, who was caressing a deep-set orange stone that hung around her neck.

Ruben led us both out of the magical house of stones and back into the warmth of the sun. The fresh air helped to clear our minds, and we looked at our stones in awe. Ruben spoke quietly, "The stones replicate the feelings you desire most, and help to suppress the unpleasant feelings that you want to ignore. Truly a wonderful gift. Okay, let me take you back to the square and I will show you where you will stay." The quiet finality in his voice said that he wouldn't answer questions.

The walk back was completely different, everything was still as beautiful, but now the buildings seemed to sing out to me and my desire for my own collection of treasures grew within me. Even the people were suddenly friendly and called out greetings as we walked past. Our colliers were praised, and we were told how beautiful we looked with them on. As often, they would flash their own colliers and we would happily grin at each other.

On the walk back, I was certain that I glimpsed Clay disappearing behind a building. My heart jumped in my chest. I had followed him enough times to know what he looked like as he moved. I was certain; it was him. Without a second thought, I began running in his direction. I heard Ruben and Leah call after me, but I ignored them.

I rounded the corner where I thought I spotted Clay, but stopped short as I found a dead-end. I scratched my head in puzzlement and wondered if I had imagined it. There's no way Clay could have come this way; he would have been trapped, and there was no other way out of here. Maybe I was seeing things, my desperation was playing tricks on me.

Leah and Ruben came puffing up to me. Ruben looked suspiciously at the wall and then curiously at me. I answered the unasked question, "I thought I saw Clay come this way." I looked at Leah, "I guess not, I must have imagined it." Leah's eyes were filled with worry as she watched me. I tried to smile and show her I was fine, but it only seemed to make her more worried and she began chewing a nail.

Ruben cleared his throat, "Ah, alright, very well. Let's continue, shall we?"

🌲 🌲 🌲

At first, I thought we were headed back out of town, but it turned out that the place we were going to stay at was along the original path we had taken. The building was interwoven with the rocky mountain and so all you could see were windows placed in a solid stone wall. Written in colourful precious stones were the name Voyageur.

As we entered, the vastness of space shocked me. Red furnishings were spread everywhere, against the black rock it gave the place an air of sophistication. I had expected more simplistic furnishings but smirked as I realised that this whole village was the furthest thing from humble.

A woman with a warm, friendly face greeted us. She had curly blond hair and a round face. She was the first lady I saw that seemed to have some softness in her. She introduced herself as Sona, Ruben's wife. Her handshake was just as strong as her husbands and all thoughts of softness disappeared.

She was lavished with so many gold pieces I wondered how she kept herself upright. A young Hercules looking boy emerged from behind her and I recognised him immediately. Ruben stood proudly next to the boy, "This is Fort, my son. He is next in line to inherit everything that we've built."

Fort smiled and shook our hands. He also wore a collier with a red stone, but his one was a lighter, more playful red than his fathers. We were shown to our rooms and I realised that Leah and I were to be neighbours. As the door opened, I was shocked to see my room had light-blue furnishings. It was exactly the same shade as my new collier. I looked over at Leah's room and saw orange was speckled everywhere.

We looked at Ruben in wonder, but he just smiled and said, "One of the perks of staying here. Now, there are some clothes on the bed, and you will notice they also match your selected colours. However, the sandals are unchanged, for that is the only thing the Prince has forbidden us to make more beautiful. That's why many of us wear longer clothes to try and hide them." He pulled up his trousers to reveal the sandals beneath.

I looked down and realised that he wore the same sandals as the men in suits. Compared to the rest of his fine clothes, it did look worn down and out of place. Ruben clapped his hands, "Alright, now that you know where you're staying, I'm afraid I'm going to have to put you to work for a bit." He called Fort over and said, "If you don't mind, I'm going to ask that you help Fort to clean some of the parade stuff. He will show you where to go."

I had so many questions running through my head, but Leah and I followed Fort wordlessly. He led us back to the square and we began helping clear the banners and decorations that were sprawled everywhere. Fort immediately moved away from us as we worked, but I found him staring at me constantly. I whispered to Leah, "Fort definitely knows about Clay. I just need some time to talk to him."

Leah nodded, "He must know something." She looked around us, "This place is amazing, but something also doesn't feel right about it. I'm not sure all this wealth is good, seems conceited. I don't think we should stay long; we should carry on moving tomorrow."

I distractedly waved away her concerns, "Sure, as soon as we find out where Clay is." I walked over to Fort. He looked like he wanted to dash away again, but I spoke to him before he could move, "So you know Clay?" Fort was tight-lipped, but a flinch in his right eye was answer enough. "Look, I'm his brother, I've been looking for him for a while now, please can you tell me where he is?"

I could see the inner fight that was going on in Fort's head. Finally, he shook his head, "Sorry, but I can't say anything."

"But why not? I don't understand why there's all this secrecy about where he is. Why will no one tell me?"

Fort battled within himself again, but he said, "All I can say is that he does not allow us to talk about other travellers. You are on your own journey, and you need to worry about yourself. But that's all I will say." He quickly disappeared from me. I followed, something told me he was headed somewhere that I wanted to be.

Although Fort moved quickly, I could easily keep up. I had tracked many things in the forest back home, so this was easy for me. He was heading deeper into the mountains and we took so many twists and turns that it worried me that I might never find my way out again. I hid up against some rocks as I heard his footsteps stop.

Trying to spy where he was but I couldn't see him. I heard whispering.

Certain this would be Clay; I broke from my hideout and ran towards the voices. Again, I came to a solid wall, a dead-end. My frustration and anger rose to the surface, I screamed into the mountains. I was suddenly angry at Clay. He was here! I know it! Why would he be playing with me like this, doesn't he know how worried and scared I am?

I walked up to the wall and beat it with my fists. Putting my back against it, I slid to the floor, breathing heavily. I grasped my collier and stared into my blue stone that had given me so much peace earlier. The blue stone drew me in again, but my anger remained knotted in my stomach. Thoughts of violence entered my mind, and it was such a shock that it knocked me out of my daze. Getting back to my feet with a groan I began my journey back. Hopefully I wouldn't find myself lost. I refused to think of what had just passed through my mind.

When I easily found myself back in the square, the light was fading, and I could see lamps were being lit everywhere. It made all the precious stones glitter and shine, but I barely noticed. I found myself still wound up from another disappointment. Leah saw the look on my face and kept quiet. We couldn't find Fort, so we headed back to the Voyageur. Declining offers of dinner I went straight to my room.

In my current mood, I didn't want to talk to anyone. I flopped onto my bed and lay there, but felt the collier digging into my chest, so I carefully took it off and put it on the bedside stand. With no energy to scream anymore, I just gave my pillow one feeble punch and buried my face in it.

I fell asleep soon after and had dreams filled with hatred. In my dreams, I destroyed the room I was in, and I knocked over the obnoxious statue in the town square. I angrily shoved Clay, and we got into a fight. Even Leah and I got into a fight that ended with me in a chokehold and her laughing.

I awoke the next morning with even more anger than before and lay in bed seething. I could see a bit of light was coming through the window, but not knowing where the sun came from also made me angry. I heard a soft knock on my door and would have ignored it, but I heard Leah's voice call out. Wanting an outlet for my frustration, I put on my collier, and then stomped to the door and yanked it open.

Leah was dressed in an inky orange dress lined with jewels. She had brushed her black hair and some darkness around her eyes had disappeared. The sight of her extinguished some of my anger. I gestured for her to enter and took a seat; I hadn't even realised I had a chair in my room. She looked at me seriously, and asked, "How are you doing? I didn't want to ask yesterday because you came back so angry, but what happened when you went after Fort?"

"Nothing happened, and that's the problem!" My voice rose to a shout, "What's the point of all this? We're just wandering around without knowing what we're doing, and no one will tell us anything useful. Clay is here! I know it! And yet, I can't find him, and he doesn't seem interested in coming to me. I don't know why I'm even bothering." I pushed my palms against my eyes to stop from crying. Again, I wondered what was in this air that made me so emotional. I focused on the ball of anger that had grown within me, and slowly the tears disappeared.

Before Leah could respond, Sona lightly knocked on the door and announced that breakfast was ready. I glanced at Leah and saw the concern in her eyes, but her concern irritated me. I flung open the door and headed to breakfast. The food tasted like ash in my mouth, and Leah's constant looks at me fuelled my desire to break something. I remembered that Ruben had mentioned mining yesterday and so I asked him, "So how does the mining work? Am I allowed to come along and help?"

Ruben beamed, "Of course you can! That is wonderful news, I am headed there myself now. You can come with me and I'll show you the ropes." He looked at Leah, "Unfortunately, mining is only for men, but you can stay with Sona and help her. I'm sure she will appreciate the extra hands." I looked over at Sona and she definitely didn't seem to need, or want, any help, but she forced a smile, anyway. Leah looked at me in desperation, but I ignored her and got up to leave with Ruben.

I quickly changed into my new clothes before we left. Ruben said it was more comfortable, and it surprised me to realise how right he was. The light blue material was light and was smooth against my skin, and even the sandals were comfortable, although I cringed as I saw them next to the expensive clothing I was now wearing. As soon as I was changed, we travelled back into the mountains and I soon heard pickaxes hammering nearby. My fingers itched at the coming work.

Ruben handed me a pickaxe and pointed at a spot in the rock, "This is a magnificent spot, usually I take it, but as it's your first day, I'll let you have it. Let me show you what you want to do." He hammered in the same spot, and rock splintered everywhere. He made it look easy and soon I spotted a glittering black stone. He motioned for me to get closer. Ruben then took a smaller hammer and chisel and began carefully digging it out. He pried it out with a smile and handed it to me, "As easy as that. Now it's your turn."

I lost track of time as I beat the rock and carefully chiselled out my prizes. The suspense of finding the next precious stone kept me going, and the hours slipped by. I was feeling the weight of the treasures in my pockets and smiled happily. The exercise helped me to rid myself of some of my anger. Each new stone made my smile come back a little stronger. Yet, when Ruben and Fort came and ate lunch with me, I could see the bulge of their stones and I realised how little I had compared to them.

Ruben encouraged me, "You will get better. A few years and you will be just as good." After lunch, they left me to continue my pickaxing.

By the end of the day, I could barely raise my arm anymore, but I was happy with how well I had done. I had emeralds of every colour and I needed two hands to hold them all. I couldn't believe how much I had gotten in one day. Fort gave me a satchel to carry them and we headed back to the house. I happily showed Leah, but she looked worried and bit her nail. I told her not to worry; soon I could buy us our own house, or one each! I will sort us out.

She tried to talk to me about Clay, but I ignored her and focused on my treasures. I continued mining for another three days, and my bounty grew. I found that my anger subsided only when I was out mining all day. Each morning I awoke with an angry ball of fire that needed to be released.

After the third day of mining, we had returned home, and I was sitting on my bed admiring my day's haul, when I heard my door open and Leah snuck in. The first thing I noticed was she was no longer wearing her collier and new clothes. She still wore the sandals, but the rest were what she had arrived here in. She put her finger to her lips and seated herself on the bed close to me, "I think we need to leave tomorrow. Something's not right about this place."

"What are you talking about?" It shocked me, "This place is amazing. Look at what I've gotten in three days. Three days Leah! Just imagine what I will have after a few months. Or even years! We can't leave, and why are you wearing your old clothes, the new ones looked so nice on you? I could give you some of my stones to add to your dress if you feel there weren't enough on them? We don't want to offend Ruben and Sona; they've been very good to us."

Leah shook her head, "Don't you see, you have become obsessed with these stones." She picked one up, and I quickly snatched it back. Leah grunted and said, "Sona told me about the parade that happened. The Prince was here! We had just missed him; we need to continue to try to get to him. I know you don't care if you find Clay anymore, but to get home we need to get to the Prince."

She indicated her clothes, "I want to leave tomorrow, and the man in the black suit told us to not take any of this place's treasures with us. That collier was making me feel sad, I'm sure it was sucking the hope out of me, so I definitely don't want that thing around my neck any longer. I kept the sandals because they just feel right… and there are no precious stones on them so it should be fine."

"I still care whether we find Clay. I just think we can learn from these people if we just stay a bit longer. Give me a few more days and then I'll come with you. I just need to stay here for a while more, I can't leave yet."

Leah's face saddened, "Please Lino, let's leave tomorrow. You won't find what you're searching for here."

"Soon Leah, I promise." My stones already distracted me. One of them was still dirty, and I was struggling to get it to shine. I didn't notice Leah leave my room.

I awoke early the next morning to whispering. I groggily tried to ignore it, but I immediately recognised the one voice. Clay was in the house! I jumped to my feet and tried to open the door quietly. I ducked back inside as I spotted Fort walking back to his room. Once I was sure the coast was clear, I left my room and walked out the front door.

In the faded light, I could see a hooded figure walking away. My heart leapt in my chest and I quickly followed. This time I was not letting him out of my sight, even if that meant he saw me. Somehow, I couldn't get closer to him and even when I sped up, he remained the same distance from me. I called out, and the figure turned, but then disappeared through a large rock arch that exited the village. I continued my chase, but as I got to the arch, I felt a giant hand scoop me off my feet.

I called out for help as I came face to face with a head that was definitely too large to be human. Green eyes gazed at me in the enormous face, and there was a nose that was equally big and a toothy grin. I struggled against the giant hands, but I was trapped. Next thing I knew, I was being lowered back to the floor and was turned to face my captor. A bit of distance between us showed me that this was indeed a man, well, a man that was double my size. He had childlike facial features with a grin that split his face as he raised his hands in a fighting posture and grumbled, "We wrestle!"

I screamed and tried to flee as he lunged for me. His arms easily wrapped around my chest and I prepared myself for the crushing pain I was about to feel. Instead, I felt the rumble of his chest and realised he was laughing. He gleefully shouted, "Escape from Fred!" I struggled against his chest, but I could not budge.

The giant man-child, Fred, laughed and lowered me to the ground again. He got back into his fighting stance and motioned for me to attack. I tried to move back out of his reach, but he moved forward and frowned, I could see he didn't like me not playing along. Since he hadn't hurt me the first time, I figured I could at least try to fight my way out.

In an uncharacteristic burst of courage, I lunged to my side, and then went for his legs. It felt like I had tried to tackle a tree. My shoulder hit his sturdy legs, and I felt his hands wrap around my mid-section. He laughed and set me down again, I could see the glee in his eyes. My collier burnt against my chest, and my anger boiled. This giant man boy was making fun of me. I pretended to spot someone coming up behind him, and as the gigantic man turned to look, I pounced on his back and wrapped my arms around his neck. He laughed as he clumsily stumbled a few steps, but then he straightened and began spinning around.

I tightened my grip on his neck, but the momentum forced my legs off his back and they propelled in the air behind me. I could feel my arms slipping from his neck and then, in desperation, I tried to change my grip and felt my finger sink into something soft and squishy. I was flung onto the ground as I heard Fred cry out and reach for his eye.

In my anger, I rushed at him again, but he plucked me up with one hand and set me down away from him. I was about to run at him again when he put up a hand to stop me and said, "Take collier off."

I looked down at my stone and found it glowing; I had never seen it do that before, but I could feel my anger intensify as I looked at it. The powerful emotion confused me, I thought it made me calmer. The enormous man still clutched his eye and looked at me with a hurt expression. I said, "I chose it because it helped me feel calm." I looked at him in wonder, realising that I had tried to fight this giant man.

He harrumphed, "It takes your happy - makes you angry. No collier, or no play."

That wasn't what Ruben had told me. He had said that it replicated the feelings I desired most. I chose it because it made me feel peaceful, not angry. Although, I realised I hadn't been peaceful at all in the last few days. If anything, I had felt angrier the longer I was here. I said, "Fine with me, I wanted to leave anyway. Just let me past and I'll go."

He shook his head, "You may not pass. Not until we finish wrestling."

My anger flared again, "Let me pass! You let my brother go past just before me, why didn't he have to wrestle you?"

"I don't wrestle Clay. Others will."

I froze, this was the first time someone had acknowledged that Clay was here, "You know my brother?"

The big man blinked his injured eye a few times and then got back into his wrestling position, "Take off collier. We wrestle."

I decided that the only way I might get some answers was if I played along. I took off my collier and lay it carefully on the ground. The weight that lifted off me as it left my neck was a surprise. In the same motion, I spun around and ran at the man. His grin split his face happily. It became a mass of limbs as I tried to get a suitable position, but he constantly beat me. The oddness of the situation made me laugh, and Fred laughed with me. I mistakenly hit him a few times and heard his grunt, but he never once hurt me back. It was as if he were wrestling a child and didn't want to injure me.

After getting tangled with myself, I stood back and laughed, Fred waited eagerly. I suddenly remembered doing this with my dad. I saw myself in our backyard, and I was wrestling him. I also could never beat him, even when Clay had joined in and we worked together. I looked around, and half expected Clay to come to my aid. The memory was such a happy one, I couldn't help but smile.

I took a deep breath and moved towards Fred again. We wrestled for a few minutes and it surprised me to find I was gaining a few advantages. I buried my face into his back and as I tried to cling to him, I felt my fingertips meet for the first time around his stomach. I yelled triumphantly and clutched tighter, but I felt my fingers get pried apart and I fell to the side.

I quickly got back to my feet and stopped, stunned. Fred was now my height, but he didn't seem to notice the change and was eagerly motioning for me to come for him. Without thinking, I charged, and we continued wrestling, now that we were more even, I won a few rounds. But each time I got up, I found that Fred was getting smaller.

After a few more rounds, all of which I won, I now found Fred to be half my height. I easily caught Fred and held him tight. A few times he accidently elbowed me painfully, but I made sure not to hurt the smaller Fred. I realised this would have been how my dad felt wrestling with us. The connection made me smile fondly. Fred started laughing as I easily held him trapped among all my limbs.

He wriggled free and stood in front of me, "Thanks for playing, Lino! Fred tired now." He flashed his enormous smile and skipped away. I called out, "Where is my brother headed?"

Fred replied over his shoulder, "To the Prince!"

I sat on the floor, dazed. I looked at Fred disappear around a corner, and it horrified me to see Leah leaning against a rock watching me. She had an enormous grin on her face as she walked towards me, "Did you have fun playing with your new friend? You look pleased for beating a small boy in a wrestling match."

"He was not that small when we started, he was twice my size!"

Leah widened her eyes playfully, "I'm sure he was."

I scowled, but then laughed, "What does it matter, I won!" I raised my fists into the air and Leah laughed with me. I walked towards my collier and was about to pick it up when I paused. I looked at Leah, "Why did you take off your collier?"

She became serious, "I can't explain it, but it felt like my collier was stealing my hope. I picked it because it gave me this glorious sense of purpose and hope, but the longer I kept it on, the more I felt my hope disappearing and it left me feeling hollow."

I stood back and looked over Bijou, the village of treasures. Something felt different, and I realised I didn't want any of those treasures anymore, I wanted to be with my family and be among people I loved. The memory of my dad and wrestling with him warmed my heart. Family was worth a lot more than precious stones. I said, "I'm ready to leave, I think we should move on from here."

Leah smiled and showed me the pile of clothes she had been holding under her arm, "I brought your old clothes with me, just in case you changed your mind."

We grinned at each other as I took the bundle from her, "All right, let me change and then let's get out of here."

Leah sighed happily, "No more sewing stupid stones onto dresses, I can do with never having to do that again."

"Poor Sona will have to do it without you now, I know how much she enjoyed your help." We both laughed, and I felt my excitement rising as we were about to get back to our journey. Clay was going to the Prince, and we were right behind him.

Poor Company

The cool of the morning had vanished and a stifling heat had taken its place, I regretted that I hadn't eaten breakfast and I was feeling its effects. My stomach growled, and I asked Leah, "No chance you brought any food with you is there?"

She shook her head, "Unfortunately not, Sona was very protective over her kitchen."

I sighed heavily; we were still walking on a small path among huge rocks and I'd forgotten how long we'd been going for. There was no chance of finding anything to eat while surrounded by rocky cliff faces. I remembered the soup that had magically appeared while we were on the hill-top, surely something like that will happen again now that we were hungry.

I stopped walking, clenched my eyes shut and began thinking about food. I focused everything I had on food appearing, and I fully expected it to be there when I opened my eyes. Yet I opened one eye, only to see Leah looking at me like I had lost my mind. I blinked my eyes a few times pretending I had some dust in them and hurried ahead of her.

The joy and excitement I had felt from continuing the journey was long gone, and I again questioned why I was doing this. Clay remained out of sight and it didn't seem like he wanted my help, anyway. We had no idea how far away the Prince would be, so it all was feeling pointless. The only bright-side I could think of were these sandals I was wearing.

Leah and I both wore plain brown sandals, but they were the most comfortable things I had ever worn. Even after all the walking we had done, my feet still felt fresh and able to continue going. However, my mind was a different story. I could feel myself dipping into a place I knew well, something I had experienced many times over my past year off. I like to see myself progress continuously, and if that wasn't happening, I would feel a lack of worth.

I realised that our brief stay in Bijou had reawakened that in me. I had loved seeing the progress of my gems and seeing the pile grow. The sense of accomplishment I felt at the sight of every new stone reminded me of my desire for more. I needed to accomplish something to feel good about myself; my achievement felt like it gave my life meaning. Now my treasure was gone, and it left me feeling hollow.

I shook my head and tried to get rid of these thoughts; I knew where they led me, and I didn't want to go back. I had a mission, and I needed to focus on it. The only distraction that I could think of that would be strong enough to take my mind off things was to think about Leah. I looked over my shoulder at her, and she flashed a smile. I glanced away and focused on where I was walking.

Despite my earlier reservations, I had to admit that having her around was comforting, and I enjoyed her company, even though she often drove me crazy. She had this carefree spirit that I found fascinating; it was different to my more methodical way of doing things. She and Clay were similar in that regard - they both had this ability to go with the flow and enjoy the moment. I was always living in the future, wishing to become a better version of myself, and I wasn't even good at that. So far, all my planning had only brought anxiety and feelings of being a failure.

Leah walked up beside me, and without thought I asked, "So how much time had you been spending with Clay?"

She shrugged, "Not much, but we would sometimes chat when we were both outside. He always made me laugh, and I looked forward to having someone to talk to." She blushed and looked away.

I nodded wonderingly and was surprised by the spike of jealousy I felt. I suppressed it roughly and said, "He has a way of finding the funny side of things." I wondered if Leah liked Clay. That would explain her insistence on coming along. When we were younger, I had a massive crush on Leah, but I had never been brave enough to do anything about it, and I had been convinced she liked Clay. It seemed like we were back in familiar territory, although, I would not allow myself to entertain such ideas. I was here on a mission and I would not get distracted.

Leah said, "I wonder how he's doing? I hope he's all right."

I tried to be comforting, "I'm sure he's fine. He's probably doing better than we are."

She laughed, "He's probably having a lot more fun. Maybe I came with the wrong brother."

I remained silent and clenched my jaw, annoyed that she would say something like that. I had never asked her to come with, and now she was wishing she was with Clay. I couldn't compete with Clay, but at least I hadn't been stuck here for weeks like he had been. The rising feeling of competition surprised me.

"Lino, I was just…"

I stopped her as I heard the familiar sound of people laughing and I signalled for her to keep quiet. Glad that she didn't have a chance to say anything else, I was happy to see that she wore a frown. My feet carried me forward as my nose picked up the smell of food. We walked around the corner and the narrow path opened up into a large open space.

We looked around for the voices and found them coming from three men who were sitting around a small fire in a cave on the outskirt of the large space. The smell of the cooking pot kept pulling me nearer. I got closer and I saw that the men were not particularly clean, and it looked like they actually lived in the cave. I saw their clothes piled in a corner that confirmed my suspicion.

Leah pulled on my arm, "Lino, let's go. They don't look friendly. Let's rather find another spot."

I shrugged her off, still annoyed, and feeling spiteful I walked toward them. I would show her just how much she would wish she were with Clay. Despite their odd home, I decided they looked harmless enough, and whatever they had in that pot was making my mouth water. Leah sighed and looked distastefully at the men, but she didn't say anything further to me.

The three men were quite young, Lino guessed late twenties. Although they looked weather worn and run-down for their age. They all were overweight, and a faint sheen of sweat was on their foreheads as they watched the pot boil. The first man wore a greasy pony tail, he looked shorter than the other two and had a happy curve to his mouth. The other two men had thick heads of hair that stood up in every direction and small faces, I realised they were twins.

They looked up as we neared them, a loud roar of greeting proceeded, and they leapt to their feet and came towards us. I could see the confusion on their faces, as I realised they must've thought I was Clay, but they clambered towards us anyway and we were crushed with hugs and pats on the back. The men didn't smell much better than they looked, but their friendly welcome lowered my defences.

We were offered seats on the floor around the fire and mister ponytail began the introductions, "My name is Soul, and these two trouble-makers are Toxi and Mane. Welcome to our place of residence. We are always happy when we have travellers come through here."

I suppressed a smile as Soul jiggled with happiness. His happiness was contagious as he continued, "We had one other fellow come through not so long ago, he was fun wasn't he, Mane?" The one twin nodded his head dreamily. The two twins looked quite dazed with lucid eyes unfocused and silly grins on their faces.

I jumped at my chance, "Did the previous traveller look like me? I'm looking for my brother, Clay."

Toxi put his finger to his lips, "We cannot say, it is Forbidden." Toxi and Mane leaned against each other and started laughing. Soul chuckled but explained, "The Prince does not like us to talk to travellers about others who have come through. Although, I've never seen two people travel together, it is rather strange." He eyed us suspiciously.

I noted the hint of distaste as Soul spoke about the Prince, him being the first one with this attitude. Everyone else seemed to be in awe of him. Leah replied, "When we arrived, we were told the Prince had given us permission to travel together." She held her head up defiantly as if daring Soul to challenge her.

Soul bowed his head in acceptance, "If the Prince said so, then it must be good." He looked out the corner of his eye at the twins, and they all burst into laughter.

Leah and I looked at each other in confusion. With a shrug, she motioned for us to leave, but I shook my head as I wanted to hear more from these men. This was my opportunity to show her that I could be fun as well, and maybe they would tell me more about this Prince. I already had my doubts about him and wanted to know more, maybe if I could keep them talking they would tell me about Clay as well, "Have you ever met the Prince? I wonder what he's like?"

The laughter had died down and they were staring at the boiling pot. As Soul took a spoon and tried it, his whole body jiggled happily again. Mane tried to steal a bite too and had his hand slapped by mister ponytail. I thought they didn't hear my question, but then Soul answered, "Yes, we have met the Prince," Again there was this dislike in his voice, "We actually saw him a few days ago, he came through here after his parade at Paradis."

Toxi piped up, "He wasn't very nice to us."

Soul looked mildly annoyed by the interruption, but he nodded, "He wasn't too nice at all. I've met him on two other occasions and both times he looked down his snooty nose at us either trying to make us go with him and leave our cave behind. We are not sheep who blindly follow anyone."

Soul looked me defiantly in the eyes and continued, "Anyway, we rejected the offer, because we know what happens to people who go to the Prince's city, and we don't want the same to happen to us." Toxi and Mane grunted agreement, and then looked eagerly as Soul took the pot off the fire. I watched in fascination as a beautiful golden liquid was poured into five mugs. The aroma that filled the air made me light-headed, and a smile came on my face, it was wonderful.

I eagerly reached for the mug and took a sip. A deep groan of delight resonated in my gut as the golden liquid went down my throat, creamy with a wild honey aftertaste. When I looked at the others in wonder, they all had the same look of pleasure on their faces, except for Leah, her mouth was tightened in disgust. Taking a second big sip with a sigh, I thought this had to be the best thing I had ever had, and nothing would ever taste as good as this ever again. All my worries disappearing by the third sip and a freedom entered my bones. I was ready to dance and enjoy my newfound freedom.

Leah had put her mug to the side and was asking, "What happens to people who go to the Prince?"

Toxi and Mane were happily sitting back to back and singing while they enjoyed their warm mugs. Soul's cheeks were flushed with happiness, as he tried to focus on Leah, "They never come back! Or if they do, they are all brainwashed and singing the Prince's praises. We don't want that to happen to us, now do we?"

I shook my head in agreement, the whole cave spun around, and I enjoyed going with the ride. I took another sip but was disappointed to find there was nothing left. Grumpily I frowned, noticing that Leah's mug was still full, I carefully switched our mugs and giggled in delight as I took another sip. I groaned with pleasure and could not fathom why Leah looked put-off by this, it was delicious. Now she was being the un-fun one, it was impossible to please her.

Leah was continuing her investigation; I didn't understand her obsession with the Prince and I continued sipping my golden heaven. Leah asked, "How do you know what happens in the Prince's city? Have you ever been there?"

Soul pulled his face away from his mug in shock, "Been in the city? I would never step foot in that place! We have many travellers come through here, and we never see any of them again. Now you tell me if that is suspicious or not."

Leah was not looking convinced and looked over at me. I pretended to be paying attention, while I could not help but take another sip. She frowned and said, "Are you alright? Your face is all red, and your eyes seem unfocused."

I nodded quickly and Toxi and Mane started giggling. They mimicked my head nodding and I saw how funny I must have looked, so I started laughing as well. Leah tried to take the mug from me, but I quickly snatched it back and emptied it down my throat. I looked triumphantly at her and everyone started laughing even more, except for Leah. I didn't understand why she was being so difficult. This was what she wanted. I would prove to her that I could be as fun as Clay. She said to me, "Come, let's go. Clay didn't leave so long ago; we can still try to catch up to him."

Soul cried in protest, "No, you can't leave! We have more. Here, fill up your mugs." I eagerly leant forward, but Leah pushed my hand away, "Lino, Clay left this place and so should we. Come, let's go."

I grumbled, "Picking him over me again. I can be fun as well."

She stood up and put out her hand for me to take. I saw the concern in her beautiful face and her soft hand was waiting for me with a smile, "I know you are fun. Just come with me."

A broad grin sprawled over my face. Leah thought I was fun – that's fantastic! I eagerly reached for her hand. My head felt fogged, but I felt a small victory. She wanted me to go with her. I felt like finding Clay and telling him that I was winning.

The Last Leaf

As I was trying to get to my feet, I heard Soul say, "Clay would've stayed with us, he wouldn't have run away after just one drink." He left the challenge hanging in the air. I felt Leah's hand tighten around mine, but I paused.

"Don't listen to him, Lino. Let's go find Clay." Leah pleaded.

"Clay! It's always about Clay with you." I knew Clay would likely be close by, but my ego was telling me to stay. I pulled my hand free from Leah and heard her sigh. I lifted my mug for another drink. Soul smiled as he filled me up.

"I'm going to get some fresh air." Leah walked out the cave.

I felt my happiness disappear with her. Glued to my mug and feeling despondent, the hollowness I had been feeling over the last few weeks came over me stronger than before. I looked around me sadly, and Soul motioned for me to take another sip. Behind the light cast by the fire, his face was filled with hunger. His smile widened as I took another sip, as soon as it touched my tongue, I felt my spirit begin to lift again and my happiness return. Another sip and I joined in the singing with the twins. We all got to our feet and danced around the fire; I couldn't remember ever feeling this happy. All thoughts and worries had disappeared.

I couldn't recall how long we danced for, but I was soon out of Miel - that's what Soul called the wonderful drink, and I could feel my mood dropping again. After three mugs, I felt my head spinning and I was starting to feel slightly nauseous. Soul told me that this was completely normal, especially for the first time, but it got better the more you had. He filled my mug again, and the first sip made all unpleasantness disappear. This stuff was amazing! I wondered where Leah had gone.

I said, "Leah always liked Clay. It's no wonder she wants to find him so bad." I joined in some hopscotch with the twins. There were no shapes on the ground, so we hopped aimlessly.

Soul was lying on his back, he said, "You don't need her, she's a bore."

I stood balanced on one leg, trying to find my next spot to hop to, "I thought she would like me if I was more like Clay. It hasn't worked so far." I looked up and yelped as the twins crashed into me.

We lay on the floor laughing, but I could already feel the last mug wearing off. We had finished the entire pot and now had to wait for more. Soul and the twins argued briefly about who would get the ingredients. Apparently, there was a place where you could collect everything. Mane lost the argument, and he grumpily walked out the cave.

The rest of us lay on our backs and closed our eyes. The brightness from the entrance of the cave was painful. My head was throbbing worse than ever and I was certain if I moved too much I would throw up. Soon I heard the other two snoring lightly, and I felt myself dozing off.

"Lino," I awoke and groaned in pain. Leah's voice came again, "Lino, Clay just came past us. If we go quickly, we can catch him!"

I struggled to my feet and tried to steady myself. I saw Mane had come back with the ingredients, but he had fallen asleep before starting the next pot. My head wasn't spinning as badly anymore, but I still felt disoriented. I couldn't believe Clay was nearby, but I stumbled toward Leah, nevertheless. I reached out to her for some balance, but she moved ahead out of reach. She motioned for me to follow her. I wondered why Clay hadn't just waited for me, why would he come back to the cave and then leave again. Thinking was painful, so I just followed Leah.

Even in my dazed state, I realised that we had been walking for a while, "Leah, how far is he? Are you sure he went this way? Maybe we should go back and wait for him in the cave?" I craved more Miel, and I imagined that it was already boiling on the fire, just waiting to be drunk. I licked my lips eagerly.

"Just a bit further, keep up."

I paused; the scenery was changing. The rocks were falling away, and it was being replaced by greenery and trees. It reminded me of our forest back home and then I realised we were heading into a forest. I heard water running nearby and birds singing in the trees, it was such a homely sound that I stifled a sob. Leah had disappeared around some trees and I looked back in the direction we had come from. For a moment I contemplated going back, but decided against it, and headed after Leah.

The smell of the woods brought back so many happy memories that I briefly forgot about my aching head. I headed toward the sound of water hoping to find Leah there. When I came out into a small clearing and found a slow-flowing stream, it was so calm and perfect that I was convinced it wasn't real. I slipped my sandals off and put my toes in the water, it was cold but refreshing. I saw that the water bank dropped off quickly and it became quite deep, one could easily swim in there.

I wondered where Leah was, but then I felt a strong shove from behind. Yelling out in surprise I tumbled into the water. The cold took my breath away and I came up spluttering and gasping for air. I coughed up some water I swallowed. Looking at Leah in shock, she stood with her arms folded angrily. My shock turned to anger, "What was that for? Are you crazy!"

She kicked some water into my face, "Why would you drink that stuff? Didn't you see what it was doing to you? How could you be so stupid! I saw an ugly side of you today that I didn't like."

As I got out the water and shivered, I could feel my head was more clear now, but I was still angry, "That's no reason to push me into the water! I was just having fun with them, you were just too stuck up to join in, that's not my fault!"

Leah quivered with anger and I thought she was going to push me in again, "Drinking will not solve any of your problems, instead it will just make everything worse."

"How would you know? That was the best I've felt in a long time."

Leah looked sad for the first time with her shoulders slouched and her arms wrapped around her body as if to protect herself form the memories, "My dad, he drinks a lot." A fire returned to her eyes, "I know what it does to people, and I promised myself I would never be with someone who abused it."

Her cheeks burned brightly, and she quickly looked away from me. I tried to figure out why she was suddenly being awkward. She snapped, "Stay here and get dry, I'm going to go find some berries or something for us to eat." With that, she marched into the forest, leaving me more confused than ever.

I had taken off my shirt and lay spread out on the grass, soaking up the last of the day's light. Although there wasn't a sun, I could still feel the warmth pulsating from somewhere. As my head continued to clear, I realised what a strong grip Soul's Miel had over me. I even found myself desiring to go back for more, even though I knew it wouldn't be good for me. The taste was amazing, and I would miss that a lot, but it was more the feeling it gave me that I was craving. The more I had, the less I thought, and for me that was a relief. I could enjoy the moment and not worry about what was coming next, I became the version of myself that I always wanted to be. I became more like Clay.

I felt bad for hurting Leah again, but how was I to know that her dad drunk a lot? This time it felt like a deeper wound had been exposed, and I hoped that she wouldn't hold it against me. I had ruminated about the last thing she had said to me, and deep down I hoped she had been speaking about me, and that she might possibly like me as well, but I didn't want to get my hopes up.

Everything was so confusing, and I'd made so many mistakes already that I didn't want to allow myself to mess this up as well. I needed to shut down my feelings and focus on finding Clay - that's what's important, not trying to find out if a girl likes me back. I closed my eyes and drifted off.

I awoke to sounds of Leah huffing as she returned into the clearing, I noticed the light was beginning to fade but I could still see the tension around her eyes and her lips were drawn thin. She sat down a short distance from me and stared at the stream as she said, "I couldn't find anything, I'm not sure what is actually edible or not, so I just left it."

I remained silent and I tried to think of something to say, some way to apologize for earlier. Although I still wasn't entirely sure I did anything wrong, I wanted to bridge the gap that had come between us. She looked so fragile with her arms wrapped around her knees that I just wanted to go to her and hold her tight. I kept revising what I wanted to say, I wanted to make sure it was perfect. Being no closer to saying anything, I saw her lay down and try to sleep. I sighed softly and hated myself for my cowardice. Laying down to sleep I tried to convince myself that I would do it first thing tomorrow. I lay down and tried to sleep.

Devon Hoole

The Flowers Who Spoke

Yet again I had a restless night and struggled with dreams that left me with feelings of dread. I knew Lino was also dreaming as I often heard him muttering in his sleep. It was still dark, but I could make out everything - it hadn't gotten fully dark through the night, as if the light didn't want to acknowledge that it was time to leave.

I had dreams of my father drinking while I hid under my bed hoping he wouldn't come looking for me. The door would burst open and he would stumble around the room calling my name. Lino appeared next to me under the bed and started singing while he downed a mug of glowing liquid and, although I beg him to be quiet, he sang all the louder.

The Last Leaf

The dream changed to me looking through a telescope hoping to find something - I didn't know what I wanted to find, but I knew I needed it. Life was meaningless without it, but every time I looked through the telescope everything went dark. Other dreams were of the Prince, his back was always to me and I knew I needed to see his face and then everything would be fine. I cried out to him, but he ignored me and would walk away.

I shivered as I remembered my dreams, I had never dreamt this much in my life. It was as if my mind was trying to process all the craziness that had happened in the last few days, and the only time to do that was when I was sleeping. I looked over at Lino, he lay on his back, with his chest rising and falling slowly as he slept. I couldn't believe that he felt this need to compare himself with Clay, they did look similar with their brown hair and strong jawline, but that's where their similarities stopped.

Clay was mischievous and he was too charming for his own good, but Lino was genuine in everything he did. You couldn't always tell what he was thinking, but he had soft caring eyes as he listened to you talk. Growing up I would always try to talk to him, but Clay would take over and Lino would shyly keep back.

Those two were inseparable, and I was quickly shut out of any games they played. As we got older, I knew that I liked Lino, but I never felt like I could do anything about it, and he never seemed interested. We only ever spoke briefly and then he would quickly leave. I don't know what came over me when I decided to hold on to him as he caught the leaf. It was more than wanting to spend time with him; I'd been searching for something for a while now and I felt that the answers lay here, in this magical place.

I took a deep breath and looked around me, drinking in the magical beauty that surrounded us. We were surrounded by so much beauty and this place really did feel like a paradise, and it even sounded like the trees were singing. I got to my feet and went to the stream to wash my face. Something about the Prince was drawing me in.

I felt strongly that he had the answers I sought after, some meaning or understanding of life that I was searching for. Before this journey, it had all become bland and boring, I needed some answers and I was sure the Prince had them. Lino wasn't so keen on the Prince; I could tell he didn't trust him and would probably avoid him if he could. Especially after those men yesterday had filled his mind with their rubbish.

I had been so furious with him yesterday; I had been tempted to leave him and continue on my own. As soon as I had tasted that golden stuff, I knew that it was not right. I had gone through a stage of my own when I had snuck into my father's liquor cabinet and tried everything. It had been fun for a while, until I found myself feeling worse afterwards.

The reason I swore off it was when my father caught me one day. I had been drinking all morning and could barely stand upright. My father had walked in and laughed, saying, "Following in my footsteps! Just like your old man. Your mother would have had a heart attack." He had picked up a bottle and started downing it.

I was certain the loss of my mother was the reason my dad drank. It was too painful for him and even marrying again had not filled the gap she left. True love was hard to replace. I barely remembered anything about my mom and since my dad refused to talk about her, I felt a part of me was also missing. My stepmom was nice, as far as stepmoms go, but it wasn't the same. A girl needed her mother.

I washed my face and looked over at Lino again, I knew I had overreacted a bit yesterday, he didn't know about my dad and his drinking, but I had been so upset to see him falling for the same trap. Drinking didn't solve anything, and I thought Lino would be smart enough to realise that.

I smiled as I heard the singing again, it was an enchanting sound that gave me a sense of excited expectation. I paused as I realised it was voices making the noise… and it was not the trees. Lino had still not stirred so I decided to investigate, for the song was drawing me in, and it reminded me of something, but I couldn't put my finger on it. I walked out the clearing and into the mass of trees.

The sound seemed to bounce off the air and I could not have guessed where the source of the beautiful melody was coming from. I walked among the trees but couldn't find anything and decided on a different tactic. I headed to the water and decided to follow that. The river here had many bends, but the tree line started a few meters away from the bank, so it was easy to walk along.

I knew I was on the right track after a few minutes, for the sound was becoming clearer. It wasn't a song, but many voices speaking in perfect harmony. The voices trailed off away from the river and I walked into the forest again. I entered a small clearing that was covered with beautiful flowers. A path led into the centre of the flowers and a small patch of grass allowed space for me to sit in the middle of all this kaleidoscope of beauties.

I walked into the middle and sat on the floor. It felt natural to close my eyes, so I allowed them to fall shut. A few deep breaths and I sighed at the sweet scent in the air. It was like walking into a perfume store, except all the smells blended perfectly together. The voices increased in strength until the sound filled every part of my being. The excited feeling became stronger and I could feel my heart rate increase in anticipation. The song carried so much purpose that I felt alive again, I knew that my only desire at this moment was to wait for whatever was to come next.

As the voices were coming to a crescendo, I began to understand the words. The hundreds of voices were eagerly calling for the light to land on them. I remained seated with my eyes closed, surrounded by voices calling for the light. At last I felt a warm beam hit me in the chest and fill my body, and all the voices groaned in pleasure. I heard movement around me and opened my eyes. I watched as the flowers began opening their petals to the beam of light that shone into the clearing.

I was mesmerised by the sight and it even looked like they were dancing in the wind. I paused as I realised there wasn't a breeze, the flowers were moving! I looked closer for the first time and noticed the faces of the flowers were moving as well. I was shocked to find that the beautiful sound was coming from them, and now they were soaking up the ray of light that landed in the clearing.

I stared transfixed as a group of yellow flowers with light brown tinges on the leaves began to move in unison. Flowers with black centres and purple petals began to dance as well. Orange, blue, white, red, every colour imaginable was interspersed in the clearing. Soon all the flowers were dancing, and their voices lifted up again. I closed my eyes and marvelled as the voices seemed to race around me, it felt like hearing a wave come and go as the song passed from one group to the next.

In perfect co-ordination, the melody began travelling in a circle around me, and continued to increase in speed, until it was happening so fast that all the voices were singing at once. No words were being spoken, but somehow, I knew they were sharing their pleasure with the light and giving their thanks. The voices slowly began to fade away, and then silence fell.

I heard a voice speak next to me, "Isn't it wonderful to be alive?"

I instinctively looked around for the speaker, but then I looked down at the nearest flower. Small eyes closed and the faintest of smiles were on the face of a beautiful white flower with a faint outline of orange on the petals. It was beautiful, I stared transfixed. Still with its small eyes closed, it spoke again, "My name is Hana. Welcome to our small meadow, we love having travellers stop and visit us."

I couldn't believe the flower was talking to me, I blurted out, "You're so beautiful."

Hana smiled briefly, "Thank you. You're also beautiful, I hope you know that."

I blushed and looked away, I couldn't believe that a flower was making me blush. I tried not to think about my looks too often, but when you are next to something beautiful it is hard not to think about your own appearance. I knew I would never be as beautiful as Hana, and I wasn't sure why I was comparing myself to her, especially since she was a flower. Without thinking, I said, "I wish I was as beautiful as you."

Hana opened her eyes for the first time, they were a sparkling blue that looked into me, "I'm sorry to hear that, it hurts when we compare ourselves to others, especially when we feel they are better than us."

Tears filled my eyes. I wasn't sure where all this emotion was coming from, there must be something in the air, but for some reason Hana reminded me of my mother. I spoke softly, "I wish my mom were around to give me advice. I miss her so much."

The tears flowed as it was the first time, I had ever said that out loud. I had tried to be strong and pretend that I was always fine, it was easy to pretend when no one ever asked how you were doing. A deeper pain was surfacing, but I could feel it ease slightly with my tears. Something I had locked away for a long time was finally being released, and I could feel the weight lifting off.

I cried for the experiences I never had, I mourned for the nurturing care I needed from my mother. Someone to talk to and ask my confusing questions to, a role model to help me through life. Someone to tell me I was beautiful and hold me tight while I cried. For the first time since her passing, I allowed myself to mourn what could have been. I cried for the life I could've had with a mother. The fun we would have had, the love we would've shared.

I had feared allowing myself to think about these things, but now they flowed, and I could feel a calming peace come upon me. I missed my mom terribly, but who knew that touching the raw wound I had feared for so long, was actually the key to my healing. My tears stopped and I sat quietly, feeling numb but also better than I had in a while.

Hana looked up at me and smiled warmly, "I want you to do something, close your eyes." I obediently closed my eyes as if it was normal to follow a flower's direction.

Hana continued, "Take some deep breaths and focus on the light warming your body."

I found it easy to quieten my mind, which was strange for me, usually it was full of thoughts that tormented me. As I focused on my body, I could feel the warmth gently hitting me in waves. Hana's voice came again, "It's important to have a focus in life. Something that is meaningful and gives you purpose. We've decided to focus on the light that comes every day, and we sing our happiness to it because we are never let down."

The symphony of voices increased as filled the space. As it quietened, Hana continued, "By looking up and focusing on something beyond ourselves, we stop competing and comparing with each other. Our common desire unites us, and we can be happy. Leah, I know you are searching for meaning in your life, but let me tell you, you will not find it among other people. If you chase happiness, you will never catch it, but if you focus on the light, then it will follow you."

I digested what Hana had said, but I still had many questions. It was all a bit vague, as it always was. I looked at her and said, "I don't know what it is that I need to focus on. How do I know if it's the right thing?"

"Truth is universal, you will know when you find it. My advice would be to go to the Prince and talk to him." With that, Hana and the rest of the flowers sighed in pleasure and closed their eyes. The magical atmosphere in the air disappeared, and I felt a profound sense of loss. I knew I was back in a normal meadow with flowers, but I would never forget this experience. I heard Lino calling my name, and a few moments later he was walking down the path. He sat down next to me and sighed, "This is a pleasant spot."

We remained quiet for a while, but then Lino looked at me sheepishly and said, "I'm sorry about yesterday. I don't know what I was thinking and I'm sorry if I hurt you."

I took his hand in acceptance of the apology and lay my head on his shoulder. "You will not believe what just happened to me," I told Lino the entire experience, leaving absolutely nothing out.

Devon Hoole

Tree of Sight

I looked over at Leah in wonder as we walked through the forest. We had spent the morning talking in the meadow. She had told me all about the talking flowers, which I was sceptical about, but I tried to look as supportive as possible. Whatever happened must have been an amazing experience because something had definitely changed in her.

She told me about the song that she heard and Hana, the talking flower, and then she had told me about her mom and how difficult it was growing up without her. She had a motivated glint in her eyes, as if there was more yet to be discovered. I had listened silently and thankfully it didn't seem like Leah wanted a response, she just wanted to be heard by someone and to share what had happened.

I felt bad for never wondering how the passing of her mom would have affected her. It suddenly struck me that I never considered that life was difficult for others. Rather, I was usually too worried about my stuff and convinced that I had it worse than everyone else.

Something had also changed between us. When Leah had taken my hand and lain her head on my shoulder, it had shocked me. I made sure that I sat completely still for the entire time, just to make sure I didn't disturb the moment and have her move away. But now, the moment had passed, and we were unsure how to engage with each other anymore.

I liked her more than I will admit, but I was unsure how to go from here. I wish I could ask Clay; he would know what I should do. This was the problem with relationships, it made you question everything and overthink every situation. I was convinced that she also liked me when we spoke earlier, but now I wasn't sure. Maybe it was because of what she experienced in the meadow, and she was so ecstatic about the situation she had forgotten herself. But what if she was interested?

I caught her eye, and we smiled at each other. I pretended to become interested in the trees around me as we carried on walking. I noticed that the trees were getting bigger, and I felt smaller with each step. The trunks were thickening, and even lower branches were getter farther away. Soon the trees had blocked out all view of the sky above and we walked under a full tree top canopy. The thickness of the canopy blocked out a lot of sound and I tried to walk more quietly. You could hear birds in the distance, but they sounded disconnected from us.

By now, Leah and I could not have gotten our arms around a tree trunk. After another ten minutes of walking, the tree trunks had grown monumentally large, the trunks being easily as big as small apartments. Unsure if we were still headed in the right direction, but clueless of where we were going anyway, we kept walking.

A man appeared from behind a tree and Leah and I both gave a yelp of surprise. It was the man in the green suit from the hilltop who smiled at us, "Welcome to Arbre, our little slice of heaven." He took a deep breath and smiled again, "I'm glad to see you made it out of Bijou, where many gets trapped with the promise of riches."

I blushed slightly, knowing how close I had come to staying. At least this man looked more friendly than the last one, I felt more at ease with the green suited man. The man continued, "I do not wish to keep you long, so I will say my piece and let you go on your way. There is a lot more to explore and see. So," he cleared his throat, "The rules for Arbre are as follows: Please don't burn it down by playing with fire."

We waited for him to continue, but he said nothing more. I looked at Leah in confusion and she looked just as puzzled. The man pulled out a beautifully carved wooden walking stick and turned to leave. Leah asked, "Wait, is that it? Surely we need to know more than that."

The man paused and looked puzzled, "More? Why would you need more? You have everything you need all around you." He grinned as he used the walking staff to show our surroundings.

Leah persisted, "Someone needs to tell us something. We're wandering around aimlessly not knowing what the purpose of all this is. You called this world Paradis, what does all this mean? Please, surely there's something more you can tell us? What about the Prince? Who is he?"

The man chuckled, "You have a lot of questions. That's good. The Prince encourages an inquiring mind." The trees rustled at the mention of the Prince. Leah huffed with annoyance and folded her arms.

I wondered why things reacted to any mention of the Prince, but another question moved me more. Leah looked ready to interrogate him further, so I quickly jumped in and asked, "Have you seen Clay come through?" I suspected the answer he would give me, but I had to try at least.

The man ignored me and spread his arms out wide, "Enjoy the forest." He walked behind a tree and was gone.

We looked at each other in exasperation. I shrugged and shook my head. Leah kicked a pile of nearby leaves as she huffed, "I hoped he would answer me. I guess we will just need to keep going and see what we can find." She looked around us and spoke softly, "The Prince will answer my question." She gave the leaves one more kick and then continued walking. I followed with a slight grin. I enjoyed seeing her like this; motivated and focused.

As we walked small twigs and leaves kept getting in my sandals, and I angrily shook my feet free. Sandals were so impractical, I wished I had my own shoes back on. All gratefulness for the comfort gone now that we were on softer ground. I heard Leah call me, "Lino, come look at this."

There was no fear in her voice, only awe. Interested, I walked over to her and found her standing in front of a massive tree trunk. The biggest one we had seen so far. As I stood in front of it, I couldn't see the end of either side, it seemed like a wooden wall. Leah was looking at an engraving, I walked over, and it read, 'Tree of Sight'.

The carving was so intricate and beautiful, I naturally reached out to stroke it. A happy pleasure rushed through my fingers and I felt a powerful desire to see what this massive tree had to offer. Leah also put her hand on the carving and smiled, "This is amazing, let's see what's at the top!"

I was already trying to figure out how we could begin our climb. I took a few steps back, but there were no low branches or any sign that we could climb. I started walking along the trunk. At first, I thought I was only walking in a straight line, but when I looked back, I could see part of Leah was hidden from my view. So, it curved, but gradually. Leah caught up with me, and we continued walking.

I felt disheartened as we couldn't find a place to climb. I realised I wouldn't recognise where we started from as all the trees looked the same. We could keep looping around the tree and I wouldn't even know it. I told Leah this, and she suggested we look out for the engraving again, so we walked close to the trunk to look for it.

I lost track of time and wondered if we would ever get back, or would we be walking around this tree for the rest of our lives? I trailed my hand along the trunk and felt a boost of motivation, for it was as if the tree was urging me to keep walking. I looked behind me and saw Leah doing the same thing. I took my hand off and continued. I got in a daze of walking and only snapped out of it when I heard Leah call me.

I walked back to her and found her touching the engraving where I must've walked straight past it. I put my hand on the writing and felt the nudge to climb the tree, but there was also another feeling, one of humour, like something funny had happened. Leah said, "I think the tree thinks it's funny that we walked around it." I got the same sense and nodded dumbly while a surge of delight came through my fingers.

I said, "I think the tree understands us." Again, a pulse flowed up my fingers and into my body, I spoke to the tree, "Were we meant to walk around seeing how to get up?" I knew the tree was laughing again, as I felt waves come through my fingers. I asked, "So how do we climb to the top?" The desire through my fingers increased for me to climb.

Leah tried, "Could we please climb to the top? Will you show us how?"

As if on cue, a loud cracking sounded around us, and we looked to our right in delight and awe. Perfectly carved wooden steps had formed out of the trunk and made their way up out of sight. We felt the encouragement from the tree, it was encouraging us to go. We happily moved towards the steps, and we began our ascent.

The going was easy, and we quickly got higher up. Despite the height, it didn't feel intimidating. Our feet landed securely on each step, and I felt wonderfully balanced. Soon the ground was lost from our view, but the steps continued arching upward. I could feel my thighs burning from the many steps, but the excitement to reach the top kept me going. I guessed about thirty minutes had passed, and then we hit the lower canopy. The dark green leaves were bigger than both my hands put together, and they had golden outlines. It was such a rich green that it tempted me to take a bite.

"Leah, look at this. I wonder if we can eat it?" I stopped as I realised that Leah wasn't behind me. I must have pulled ahead of her during the climb. I had been so engrossed in getting higher, I had forgotten to see whether she was keeping up - not a very gentlemanly thing to do. I should have been more aware of where she was and slowed down if I was going too fast.

I sighed at my tactlessness and sat down, waiting for Leah to catch up and apologise for racing ahead. As I was getting comfortable, the sound of dripping water caught my ear. Curiously, I got to my feet and followed the sound. Just around the corner, I found one of the enormous leaves dripping water. As I thirstily drank, the feeling of the cool water run through my body and I felt an immediate sense of refreshment and a boost of energy urging me to continue. The desire to keep climbing burned within me.

I waited for a few more moments and then decided to carry on. Who knows how long I would have to wait for her, and maybe the top wasn't worth it? Then I could come back and prevent her from having to climb all the way up. I watched the water dripping and figured she would find the water, as there was no way to miss it running over the steps.

Having decided, I continued climbing. I noticed the stairs were changing, they were no longer easily carved out steps, but they were morphing back into branches. After a few more minutes, the steps had disappeared, and I was having to climb among the branches. The path was still obvious, and the climbing had many options to choose from. I felt bad for leaving Leah, but the pulse from the tree to keep climbing was getting stronger and I couldn't help but continue. Sweat had broken out on my forehead, my thighs were burning, and my arms felt jelly-like. I knew I would need a break soon, and hopefully I could find more water.

Then, out of nowhere, I saw the first bits of light coming through the foliage above. I felt a breeze tickle my face, and I knew I was close. I doubled my efforts to reach the top. I reached a thick branch that had wooden pieces that formed a ladder going up it. I eagerly climbed the ladder and when my head broke through the top, light assaulted my eyes.

At first, I thought I had gone blind, but then my eyes slowly adjusted. I stood on a small wooden platform; a carved wooden railing ran around its small perimeter. I looked around and saw the entire forest canopy around me. It looked as if one could walk on it. I walked to the railing and noticed that many eagles were intricately carved into it, some in flight, others perched on a tree, some feeding young ones.

The detail was breath-taking. I immediately wanted to tell Leah about it. I realised that I had no idea how far behind she was, and how selfish I had been to carry on alone. The realisation took the joy out of the breath-taking sight, it wasn't as fun accomplishing something without being able to share it with someone.

I looked in the distance and saw the beginning of a desert. I strained my eyes and thought I saw a line of spots moving. Unable to make out what it was, I turned my attention back to the small platform. Right in the centre, I found a small pool of water resting on the hollowed-out top of a branch. I eagerly took a few sips;

it was just as sweet as before and I took some deep gulps.

As I was drinking, I heard a great rush of wind and then a heavyweight landed on the platform. I spun around and backed into the railing as I came face to face with the biggest eagle I had ever seen. About the size of a man, it perched on the railing, staring intently at me. It had golden eyes that shone with intelligence, and I saw the faint glisten of gold under the wings, while the rest of the body was brown with slivers of white between the feathers.

Filled with fear, I was frozen as the eagle hopped off the railing and landed softly on the platform. Slowly it walked towards me. I couldn't have called for help even if it would have helped, so I just watched it approach. As the large eagle stopped by the water and bent its head to drink, its eyes never left me.

I squeaked, "Please don't eat me."

The large eagle spread its wings. The wingspan went off both ends of the platform and the eagle lifted its head in a screech. I hid behind my arm and waited for the attack. After a few moments, I realised that the noise coming from the eagle sounded a lot like laughing. I cautiously looked at it and saw that the eagle was looking at me with its beak opened in a smile like fashion.

The voice that came from the eagle nearly made me fall over the rail. It was deep and spoke clearly, "I have no desire to eat you young one. The forest provides all that I need. I am Absaar, welcome to my lookout."

I forgot my fear. It was now replaced by incredulity, "You can talk? How's that possible?"

I seemed to have offended Absaar, as if a giant talking eagle was the most natural thing in the world. He responded, "I learnt like any other. Now, where is your companion? I do not see her here with you?"

I was at a loss for words, "She is coming, she fell behind."

Absaar tilted his head and watched me with one large golden eye. I felt like it was seeing right through me. His deep voice said, "I see." He turned and leapt graciously back onto the railing. I noticed he was looking at the desert. I hesitantly approached him and asked, "Do you know what that small line of dots walking along the desert are?"

Absaar ruffled his feathers and said, "Yes, they are travellers, like you. They are journeying to the Prince."

Eagerly I asked, "Would you be able to tell me if you can see someone who looks like me? I'm looking for my brother and it's possible that he might be there already."

A golden eye swung towards me, and then back at the trail of people, "Sorry young one, all humans look the same to me." I sighed but hadn't expected an answer, anyway.

Absaar's penetrating golden eye focused on me again, "Why did you leave the female behind?"

My mouth worked, but no sound came out, the question shocked me, I mumbled, "I wanted to get to the top."

"Well, you made it."

I scratched at the rail, feeling embarrassed and guilty. I didn't know what to say, and I was ashamed of leaving Leah. As Absaar had bluntly pointed out my abandonment, it suddenly dawned on me how often I did this. If someone couldn't keep up with me, I would leave them behind and continue by myself. My life was interspersed with people coming and going, mostly because I wouldn't bother keeping them around.

I had done this to Leah before, just differently. When she left to be home-schooled, I had stopped trying and had left her to herself. Life was simpler alone; it was easier to avoid complications when you did things yourself, but what was the point if you didn't have anyone around at the end to enjoy it with.

Absaar continued as if he read my mind, "It's lonely at the top if you don't have anyone to enjoy it with."

I half-heartedly tried to defend myself, "But when I get to the top, I can then help others."

Absaar's one eye widened slightly, and I realised he was raising his eyebrow at me, "Is that so? How are you any help to the girl now?"

I knew he was right; I was no help up here, as she was still struggling up and I could do nothing from my position. This was bigger than climbing a tree. The framework of my life seemed to shatter. I had convinced myself that isolation was fine because I would eventually reach a place where I would be important enough to help others. Once I figured out what I wanted to do and reached a level of success, then I could help others. Once I had fixed all my own issues, then I would become more outward focused.

Now I realised that it wasn't about reaching the top, but it was about walking with others and helping them get there too. I looked around at the beautiful scenery I was standing above. I was at the top of the world and yet I felt hollow, the pleasure had been short lived and now I wished I had someone here with me.

The giant eagle ruffled his feathers and adjusted his talons on the railing, "We who are strong need to be patient with the weaknesses of those who are not, and we must stop trying to only please ourselves. The Prince told me that. He is very wise." The tops of the trees all ruffled, and the leaves sounded like they were clapping in agreement.

Despite my dislike for the Prince and not trusting him, I knew this was something I needed to listen to. Tears filled my eyes as I realised how selfish I had been in my life. I wiped my face and cursed this place for making me emotional again. My intense focus on doing well, meant that I often walked away from friendships if I felt frustrated by their issues, or when others were sluggish in understanding me. I determined to find my own way of getting things done.

At the end of my school career, I had done extremely well, but I felt a hollowness. I had no one to celebrate with, and no friendships I valued. That was probably part of the reason I relied so heavily on my bond with Clay, I needed at least one person I connected with in order for me to survive. I missed Clay more than ever and my desperation to get to him increased. My tears were gone, but my voice still croaked, "I'm sorry, I didn't mean to be like this."

Absaar's deep voice was comforting, "Sometimes journeying with people through their pain is more rewarding than achieving all your own goals. You have something to offer people, don't let your fear make you hide away."

His words cut right into my heart; I knew that was the genuine reason I kept people at a distance. I was terrified of getting close to people, only to disappoint them or have them become bored with me. No one could hurt me if I left them first. Even if it was painful being alone, at least I didn't have to face the pain of someone leaving me. I gripped the railing as hard as I could while I battled with my emotions.

This was the part of me I didn't give voice to, and I had tried all my life to bury deep inside, but now it was all bubbling to the surface. I knew I couldn't avoid it any longer, but I needed to be brave and face it. I asked him, "What if it doesn't work and I still find myself alone?"

"Then you try again. Life is empty without relationships, and just like with our kind, you humans were created to be among each other. It's not good for you to be alone, even if it feels easier at the time. Be bold, be brave, you have a lot to offer your friends."

I nodded slowly as I processed everything. I turned to Absaar, and his golden eye focused on me while I said, "I'll try."

With that, he let out a loud screech of triumph and leaped off the platform. His massive wings spread gracefully, and he soared off. The sudden departure was as shocking as his arrival, and I was left watching him float away until I couldn't make him out anymore. I had so many questions, but now he was gone. Why did everyone do that here? They left you with a million questions and then refused to answer you, or mysteriously disappeared. I sighed, but my mind was still racing with what he had revealed to me.

I headed toward the ladder determined to reach Leah and journey the last stretch with her, but as I got there, her head popped up and she smiled wearily at me. I led her to the water, and she leant against the post as she drank.

She took a deep breath and said, "That was quite the climb, I'm exhausted." The water's refreshing powers seemed to kick in and she got to her feet to look at our surrounding. She whistled in awe and walked the perimeter of the platform. I watched her graceful movements and couldn't help smiling at how happy I was that she had made it.

My talk with Absaar came back, and I said, "I'm sorry I left you behind. I should have waited, and it was selfish of me."

"Don't worry about it." Leah absently waved my apology away, she asked, "I thought I heard voices as I was climbing the ladder."

I took Leah by the shoulders, "I spoke to a giant eagle and it was amazing." I pulled her into a hug and said, "I'm so happy you are here. Thanks for being here with me." She nodded into my shoulder and I pulled her tight. The joy of having her with me and the realisation of how much I needed her, filled me with warmth. I remembered all the fun we'd had growing up together and how my heart had leapt every time she'd smiled. I appreciated that she had always been there; many of my greatest memories included Leah. How could I have missed it? How could I have tried to throw something like this away?

However, we now stood in this foreign world, chasing after my brother, and we were on the same side. We were together in this. Without thinking, I turned her head towards me and lightly kissed her. My heart soared at the feeling of her lips on mine. Her body softened into me and time slowed. This was something I had dreamt of doing since we were kids. The world ceased to exist around me as everything became focused on this moment. We broke apart, and I watched her reaction. Everything had happened so quickly, I had forgotten to think this through. What if she became angry?

A dazed smile was on her face, and she was looking at me in wonder. A mischievous glint entered her eyes, and she said, "What did that eagle say to you? It must've been quite something to get that reaction out of you."

My tension broke, and I laughed, "He helped me realise that it was good to have people around, and life is empty when you journey alone. That's why I'm so happy you are here with me, even if you've done nothing but cause trouble."

Leah laughed and lightly pushed my shoulder. She brushed past me and looked over the desert, "A talking eagle… Who would've thought? Seems unbelievable."

I knew she was teasing me for my earlier unbelief, so I stood next to her and said, "Well, it's more believable than talking flowers." We both laughed and contently stood side by side overlooking the vast environment.

🌱 🌱 🌱

The going back down felt a lot faster, and I stayed with Leah the whole way. We were both feeling giddy and happily chatted. I could feel myself beginning to feel more comfortable with her and my defence was dropping further. We spoke about whatever was on our minds and it felt like we were kids again returning from an adventure. I couldn't help but constantly steal glances at her and smile at everything she said. My cheeks were hurting from the constant smile that was lodged on my face.

Even the great tree seemed to sense our happiness, and at the bark's every touch we were filled with giddy pleasure. All tiredness from the journey to the top had disappeared and we practically skipped all the way down. Back on the wooden steps, we walked side by side, and I was sure the steps had widened just for us.

Leah was excitedly talking about the desert we had seen. I had told her that Absaar had said that the small dots were people walking and they were heading towards the Prince. She was talking animatedly, "Imagine if we are close! We could be maybe a day or two away from meeting the Prince. How wonderful will that be?" She laughed in delight.

I smiled at her enthusiasm. I was still hesitant about the Prince, but I didn't want to spoil her good mood. I was also sceptical about getting there soon. Judging from the journey so far, I didn't want to get my hopes up. I wanted to be as realistic as possible for anything that could come next. Now that I had committed to seeing out this journey with Leah, and not begrudging her company, I felt this heavy burden and responsibility to protect her. I knew this was crazy and I would never mention these feelings to her.

She would most likely accuse me of thinking her soft, but it was something I couldn't shake. I knew I would do anything to keep her safe, and it made me terrified; she had snuck into my heart and I hoped she would never leave. My admittance of my feelings for her filled me with fear, but I remembered Absaar's words and wanted to be brave. The thought of her lips on mine was also a feeling I could not shake, and I wished I could kiss her again.

We reached the bottom of the steps and it shocked me to see how dark the forest had gotten. I hadn't even noticed the darkening around us; I had been so immersed with thoughts of Leah. It couldn't be that late, but the thickness of the trees made everything gloomier and darker than usual. We decided to find somewhere to spend the night.

Before we said goodbye to the majestic tree, I put my hands on the trunk and asked, "Do you know a good place we could spend the night?" I looked down at the twigs and leaves around my feet, "Preferably something less poky." I felt the joy shoot through my arm, and a nudging pulse to take a look around the corner. Leah and I looked at each other wonderingly and began our search.

Instead of seeing the never-ending wooden wall, we saw a beautifully carved door laced with fine symbols and etched designs of nature. Carvings of trees that looked as real as the ones around us, small woodland animals playing in the leaves, and even owls sitting contently in their small caverns. I was happy to see the large powerful wings of Absaar overarching the entire door.

He seemed to welcome us in, but simultaneously protecting the way from intruders. Without further thought, I pushed open the door. We were met with the warmth of a small house and the glow of lights that hung on the walls. I wondered how they remained alight, but got distracted by seeing that everything was wooden. The home appeared to have been carved into existence. It was one with the tree and fit perfectly in, as if the tree had grown this way.

The longer I looked the more I noticed. A grand wooden table, that suggested it had grown out of the ground, was placed in the centre of the room with a bowl of multi-coloured fruit. The table was surrounded by three equally grand chairs. A lounge area was placed off to our left, and I was shocked to find a bookcase with a few books placed inside.

Off to the right looked like a kitchen, with a few cupboards and two sinks. I walked to the tap and turned it on, water gushed out. I greedily took some sips while Leah walked to the table and took a bite of a fruit. Her face was alight with awe and she took another bite, "Lino, you need to taste this! It's amazing!"

I took one for myself, it was the greenest apple I had ever seen, and as soon as the first piece was in my mouth, I felt the sweet juice run down my throat. I groaned in pleasure and saw that Leah was already on her second plum. I had forgotten how hungry I had been, but now I ravenously took more fruit. I ate things I never recognised, the strangest of which was a blue triangular fruit, but they all tasted just as good. I wanted to try one of everything. I was stuffing my mouth with a red fruit that I didn't recognize, but it reminded me of red liquorice, when the front door burst open.

Leah and I both spun around and at the entrance was the most handsome man I had ever seen. He was tanned and well-built, he reminded me of Tarzan with a strong jaw and hazelnut eyes, he was breathing heavily and quickly shut the door behind him. He wore light clothing that I imagined blended in well with the forest setting. He seemed to be looking through a small peephole in the door. After a few moments he sighed and seemed to relax. He turned around and spotted us, but instead of looking surprised he was delighted.

He exclaimed, "Friends! Welcome!" He eagerly came forward and gave us each a monstrous hug. I jealously watched as he fussed over Leah and her mouth hung open as he herded her to a chair. He motioned for me to sit and I grudgingly obliged.

He looked at us and smiled even more broadly, his perfect teeth glistening in the light, "My name is Gai, I'm so happy to have you here with me. It's been a long time since I've had travellers come along my path."

I was just about to ask after Clay, but now I knew the Tarzan man hadn't seen him. Why hadn't Clay come this way? I had forgotten how big this forest is. Clay could be anywhere. I watched Gai as he talked animatedly and wondered if he would tell me about Clay. He certainly liked to talk.

Gai continued, "Any chance you climbed the Tree of Sight? It's so wonderful!" He clapped his hands. I couldn't help but get caught up in his happiness. Joy seemed to be pouring out of his every pore. I wanted to dislike him because of the way Leah was staring, but I couldn't help myself. He seemed great.

I saw Leah wasn't in a space to answer, she still had a glazed look, so I spoke, "Yes, we did climb it, we wanted to make sure we were still headed in the right direction. Leah spotted the carving on the tree and asked it how we could get to the top. Then some steps had appeared for us to climb." I didn't mention talking to Absaar, I didn't want to look foolish in front of Gai, I wasn't sure if any of today's events were normal. Although, by the looks of him, Gai wasn't so normal himself.

Any doubts I had were quickly squashed as Gai ran his hands fondly over the wooden table and seemed to be talking to himself, "She must like you; the Tree of Sight doesn't let just anyone climb her." He looked at us with such joy, I couldn't help but grin stupidly back.

He leapt to his feet and danced along the room with his hands along the walls while saying in a sing song voice, "There's nothing quite like the beauty of nature. She's so alive and wonderful." The whole tree seemed to shake with his touch, and I worried that the entire place was about to fall in.

I steadied myself on the table and was shaken by the wave of emotions that came through my hands. I became overwhelmed by the pulses that rushed up my arms and I realised that the tree was dancing with Gai. They were lost in a duet amongst themselves. And then just as quickly as it started, there was silence and Gai fell backwards and lounged on a couch happily.

I yawned and Gai leaped back to his feet, "Where are my manners. You must be tired from your journey. Please let me show you to your rooms, we have plenty of space." I looked at Leah, but she appeared wide awake. I gave her a questioning look, to which she said, "I'm fine for now, I'm not tired yet."

Feeling a bit hurt I followed Gai into my new room. It looked exactly like the rest of the house, all made from carved wood, with a giant bed in the centre of the room. Wooden beams were at all four corners of the bed and I noticed Absaar's large wings spread out above.

Gai happily showed me the place and said, "I thought you would appreciate this room. You've had a big day and this room is for the brave among us." He patted me on the shoulder and left me to myself. I tried to fight my jealousy down and keep it under control, but I couldn't help entertaining the thoughts. He was so much better than me, I couldn't compete with someone like this. Leah was already looking at him in a way she never looked at me.

I knew I was overreacting, but I couldn't help myself. I couldn't bear to lose Leah, not after feeling like we were connecting. I walked around the room and tried to think rationally. Nothing had happened, I was imagining things. I tried to think of what Clay would do. He would fight for what he wanted. I groaned and knew that I couldn't do something like that. I told myself, "Stop this. You are being stupid."

The part of me that feared this would happen, was judging me and telling me that it had been right, as it always was. People always left me and found someone better. Flinging myself onto the bed and burying my head in the pillow with my heart bursting, it felt like my heart was bursting out of my chest. My whole body was being constricted by fear, and I felt trapped.

This is why you don't get close to people! I wanted to shout at myself for getting tricked into opening my heart. People always left. Clay being gone and now Leah, it was too much for me, I didn't want this to happen again. I focused on Absaar's words and tried to remind myself to be brave.

I lay buried in the bed and hardened my heart. I convinced myself that I was fine. I didn't really like Leah or need her, it had all been part of the craziness of the day. I would soon find Clay and then everything would go back to normal. I would be fine. I fell asleep into a deep slumber while fighting with my heart. I dreamt of Leah and Gai all night long.

I awoke in a foul mood. Mixed in with everything else that I was feeling, I was angry that I allowed this to get to me. I felt that I had turned an important corner when I spoke to Absaar, but it seemed nothing had changed. This is what grated me more than the jealousy, it felt like a better version of me had been promised and then snatched away at the first signs of tension.

Nobody else was up yet, so I stalked to the kitchen to find something to drink. No fires allowed in Arbre meant that I couldn't heat up anything, so I took a beautifully carved wooden mug and filled it with water. I noticed that the lights had come on as I walked into the room and wondered what powered them. The light appeared to float in the lanterns.

I walked over to the lounge and looked at the books on display. The covers were all in different colours but none of them had any writing on the outside. Putting my mug down, I opened one of the copies. Have I forgotten how to read?! The words were shaped similarly to ours, but my eyes wouldn't remain on a word long enough for me to read them. I realised that it was written in a different language, but I still felt that if I could just focus my eyes, then I would understand it.

I skimmed a few pages, but that didn't change the fact that I couldn't read any of it and my eyes continued to slide across the words. I sat down on one of the couches and sulked in silence. Everything was adamant about keeping its secrets. Even the books refused to give any answers.

I contemplated going outside to explore, but I didn't feel like getting lost. In any case, I didn't have to wait long before Gai came bounding into the room. He was full of energy as usual and was dressed in light green cloth. He smiled at me and launched himself onto the couch.

His energy dampened my mood even more, for his happiness and confidence came as a slap in the face.

Without pausing, Gai said, "It's a wonderful morning. You and Leah are going to have a heroic journey today. The trees are also in a good mood." He watched me as if I were going to join in his enthusiasm, but I remained quiet and only nodded. I had nothing against Gai, but presently I didn't feel like talking much or pretending to be excited about the upcoming journey.

Gai's expression turned to one of concern, "What's wrong?"

I looked away, "I'm tired. It's been a draining journey."

Gai nodded solemnly, but then his face split into a smile again, "Leah told me about your journey so far. What an exciting adventure! Oh, how I wish I could come with you." He gazed dreamily off into the distance.

"I'm only doing this to find my brother. Once I get to him, we will be out of here and back home."

A sad look passed over Gai's face as he looked at me, but it was quickly replaced by his smile, "A hero's quest. Even better!" The brief moment of sadness surprised me; I didn't think Gai was capable of emotions other than happiness. Why would he feel sorry for me?

I didn't have time to think further, because Gai had leaped from the couch and was at the door. He was looking through the little hole. I was overwhelmed by his constant activity; it didn't seem like he could sit down for long. He nodded his head happily and said, "The coast is clear, I think it would be a good time for you two to carry on your journey."

At that moment, Leah had stumbled out of her room. Despite my foul mood, I suppressed a smile at the state of her hair, I was convinced she wrestled her pillows during the night. No natural sleeping positions would cause that amount of chaos.

She yawned as she said, "Why do we need the coast to be clear? Is there something out there?" I suddenly remembered how abruptly Gai had come into the house and shut the door. It had definitely seemed like he was running from something. The shock of seeing him had made me dismiss the warning that had gone off in my head.

However, Gai smiled charmingly and spread his hands as if in defeat, he said, "My apologies, I thought you knew." He stood up straighter and puffed out his chest, "As protector of the forest, I am in charge of making sure no fires are started or anything untoward is taking place in Arbre. There is a group of misfits who are constantly challenging me and trying to cause trouble. But fear not! I always catch them. Last night, they tried to follow me home to see where I live, and so I had to use some evasive tactics to get rid of them." Gai hid behind his hands and then spied us with one eye before hiding behind his hands again.

I stared at Gai. I was now convinced that he was mentally unstable. Leah also seemed to be hiding a grin as she looked at the floor. Gai continued his explanation, "That's why I would appreciate it if you were to leave unseen. And if by chance you cross their path, I ask that you do not reveal where I live." He was already herding us toward the door. He grabbed two apples and handed them to us on our way out. He took one last look in either direction, flashed a smile and then wished us farewell. The door was closed firmly in our faces, and any proof of an entrance disappeared. We were left staring at a wall that was once again solid.

Leah's Captivity

Leah looked at me in confusion and still appeared to be half asleep, "What was that all about? Did you say something to upset him?"

I angrily looked at the tree trunk, as if daring it to reveal the door again, "I didn't say anything. I just told him I was looking for Clay, and then he said the coast was clear and that we should leave." I was annoyed that Leah assumed I had said something wrong. Gai was crazy, and who knew how his mind worked. I didn't like that Leah was taking Gai's side. I grumbled, "Whatever, let's go."

Leah wouldn't let it go, "Just think, there must've been something. I'm sure you didn't mean it. You were upset last night and maybe Gai could tell."

I spun to her. I couldn't hold in the anger anymore. I felt hurt and I wanted her to experience my pain. She stepped back in fright, I could feel the fire burning in my glare, "Go back to him then! I'm sure he will be happy to have you back." I could see the hurt in her eyes, but I couldn't stop the tirade, "I saw how you were looking at him, and I knew you would choose him over me."

Leah's hurt expression had turned angry, "I'm here with you, aren't I?! It's not my fault you felt threatened by him."

I barked a cold laugh, "You're only here because you have nowhere else to go, and no one is willing to put up with you." I regretted it as soon as the words came out of my mouth.

Tears sprang into Leah's eyes and her hand covered her mouth in shock. The pain on her face filled me with guilt and I said, "I didn't mean that." She shook her head and took a step away from me. I felt like I was losing her with every step she took. I tried to stop her, "Leah…"

She turned and fled. I called after her, but she ignored me. I cursed myself for being so stupid and insensitive. I knew how much she struggled with feeling accepted and now I had thrown it back into her face. I rushed after her, but there were so many trees that I lost sight of her. I looked around anxiously, hoping to catch a glimpse of Leah, but she was nowhere to be found. I kicked a pile of nearby leaves and berated myself for hurting her.

"Leah!" There was no response. I was alone in the quiet forest. The trees watched in disgust as they towered over me. My anger was gone, and I felt smaller than ever. What had overcome me? Where was all this anger and jealousy coming from? I never used to lose my temper, and now I had hurt the only person who was willing to help. Thoughts of Clay filled my mind, but I roughly pushed them aside. I didn't want to think about him. The leaves rustled as a gust of wind ripped through the forest. I was pushed back a step and wondered what that had been.

Leah screamed.

My heart pounded as I heard the nearby scream and sweat broke out across my entire body. It came again a few seconds later. Leah was in trouble. Another gust came and I was pushed in the direction of her voice. I began running.

Tears obscured my vision, but I continued to run. I needed to get away from Lino and I didn't care where I landed up. My heart was throbbing in my chest and my thoughts were scattered. I didn't know what just happened, or why Lino was so angry, but I needed some time to think and be by myself. I heard Lino call me, but I continued running.

A few small branches whipped me across the face, and I stumbled over something on the ground. It felt as though the forest was fighting against me as well. Lino's anger had completely taken me off guard, and I didn't know what I did wrong. Everything had been going so well yesterday, and I felt like we were going to be fine from now on. We had finally admitted how we felt about each other in the kiss we shared, and we had a meaningful conversation where we opened up to one other. That was why this hurt even more, I had not expected it to turn ugly so quickly.

Distracted by my thoughts, I realised that I was about to run into a small tree. I gave a shout of fright and swerved at the last second, but I tripped over a low branch. Face down on the forest floor, I remained still, with no fight left in me and no energy to get back up. A tinkling sound of laughter came behind me, but I was too tired to give it any notice.

Tears streamed down my face and I was reminded of the day I was told my mother had died. I had lain on my bed and felt my pillow dampen with my tears. It was the worst day of my life and all I had wanted was for my dad to hold me and tell me he loved me. But he had never come. Later that night, I had gone in search of him. I had found him passed out on the floor. Never had I felt so alone in my life. The pain and sense of abandonment I felt had stuck with me ever since. It was something I could never recover from, and now that familiar feeling was coming back.

The sound of laughter came again, and I felt rough hands grip me. I screamed out as they pulled me to my feet. I struggled to get free, but the hands were too strong. I screamed louder as I saw the men who held me. There were four of them and all were severely underweight. Their faces were sunken with eyes darkened from lack of sleep.

I couldn't tell who was speaking, but a raspy voice was saying, "Hold her tight, don't let her escape."

Another one spoke, "Keep her quiet, we don't want the forest protector finding us."

"Let her go!"

My spirits rose as I heard Lino's voice. The surrounding men cursed, and their grip loosened. I took my chance and tried to escape, but a sharp pain burst up my ankle and I tumbled over. As I fell, I saw one of the men move impossibly fast and strike Lino across the face. He fell to the floor in a heap. I screamed out to him, but I was hauled back to my feet and they forced a black hood over my head. I struggled against them but all four had me, and despite their ragged look, their grips were strong. I began to shiver in fear as I was carried off. I hoped that Lino was fine, he hadn't moved since being struck.

I lost track of time as I was dangled between the men. None of them spoke, making me become disoriented and confused. The unknown and fear of what was happening kept me shaking. I was sure I was losing my mind and if I spent any longer being blind, I would snap. I felt my fear turning into an uncontrollable panic as they dropped me onto the floor. I landed with a cry of pain as my hood was taken off. I prepared to fight and do whatever was necessary to survive. No attack came and I fell back breathing heavily.

My eyes began to focus, and I took in my new surroundings. I realised we were inside a large tree trunk, but instead of being beautifully crafted and one with nature, this was ignorantly hacked into existence. The tree was dying, and holes were forming everywhere, and instead of a door, there was a large gap that had been ripped open. After the Tree of Sight, I felt saddened by my new surroundings. No furniture or rooms were visible, and it looked like the men slept on the floor. Everything was black and there was a smell of smoke in the air. I realised that this tree had been burnt and everything inside must have been destroyed.

The men were huddled together in a circle and whispered furiously to each other. Their voices rose as they continued. They were upset about something. I took deep breaths to calm myself down, but I strained to hear them. The one with the raspy voice was speaking, he appeared to be the leader. He was thin and had a gaunt face with sharp eyes that flickered across the room as he spoke, "This is a disaster! How did this happen?"

The man next to him stood in a hunched fashion and rubbed his hands in front of his chest nervously, "How were we to know there would be more travellers in the forest, we watched the last one leave yesterday, and that means we should've had a week before the next one came."

The leader shook his head angrily, and looked at the other two, "You were on watch duty, you should've noticed new travellers had arrived."

I was shocked to see the one man burst into tears as he apologized, but the other man shrugged, seemingly disinterested in what was happening. The leader shook with fury, "Cri, stop wailing! Tristan, you were in charge and I'm holding you responsible. You know we're not allowed to touch the travellers and now we knocked one out and have another held hostage."

The man rubbing his hands nervously said, "Brennan, we thought it was Gai coming around the corner, surely we won't get in trouble for a mistake. We can also say that we were defending ourselves against the other one. He looked vicious enough." He looked nervously at the other two for support. Cri was sobbing, and Tristan had completely lost interest in the conversation.

Brennan tried to control his anger, "Brone, you are right, we will have to come up with something. Maybe this can still work for us. If Gai finds out, he will try and get her back, and that will be our chance to trap him. We need to come up with a plan that will work." He looked lost in thought, and then he shivered, "But for now, we need to get warm. Why is it always so cold in here?" He stalked to a pile of wood and yelled, "Someone make me a fire!" Brone and Cri leaped into action, while Tristan slowly walked in obedience.

The leader, Brennan, saw me watching and walked towards me while I scurried back but was blocked by the wall. He knelt down in front of me and tried to put on a caring face, but it came across as pained. He said, "Sorry for all the shouting. My friends over there are incompetent, and they only respond to strong leadership."

I pleaded, "Please let me go. I won't tell Gai what happened, just let me go."

Brennan barked a laugh, "I'm not scared of the so-called forest protector." He belied himself by looking over his shoulder nervously.

I felt some fight return and said, "Is that what you tell yourself? You need to help your friends though; they seem pretty terrified."

He laughed again, "Well, I told you they are incompetent." With lightning speed, he reached out and grasped my ankle. Pain exploded up my leg. He continued speaking in a casual tone as he said, "Don't test me. I'm after Gai, not you. So…" He flashed a yellow smile at me, "We need you to wait here quietly, and not cause us anymore trouble. Did you see what we did to your friend?"

I nodded.

He smiled again, "Good, so you know that we are serious and will not tolerate any disrespect. If you try to escape, we will find you. This is our forest, and we know everything about it, so there is no way you will get away from us." He patted me on the knee and got up, "Good girl."

I shivered as I watched him walk away. I flexed my ankle and found the pain was gone. How had his touch caused so much pain? His hands were icy, and it had spread through my body. I wrapped my arms around myself and wished that I were nearer the fire. The four men were huddled as close as they could get, and no one was talking.

Despite the light outside, it felt dark and heavy inside the burnt tree. Still shivering, I stared at the dancing flames that seemed to draw me in and leave me transfixed. Instead of feeling warmed by the sight, I felt a deeper chill go into my body and a heaviness settled on my shoulders. Dark thoughts began swirling around my mind and I slumped as my energy disappeared.

I knew something was wrong, but I couldn't motivate myself to do anything about it. I felt like the man, Tristan, and was sure I could only move at a slow pace. Tears welled up in my eyes and I felt emotional, I lay on my side and stared numbly at the flickering flames. Life always felt difficult, and there always seemed to be things that went wrong. I couldn't help but think of how much I'd been through already, and I was still so young.

I dreaded to think of what was still going to happen in my life. My stomach started churning at the thought. The weight of life and needing to carry on became a burden I didn't want to carry. I missed my mom more than ever and wished she were here with me. What was the point of all this if you just struggled through life and then died? Surely, there must be more. My eyes fell closed.

"Excuse me." I struggled to open my eyes, and they remained shut. The speaker came again, "Excuse me."

I looked up and saw the teary looking fellow kneeling nearby and pretending to be gathering sticks. If I remembered correctly, his name was Cri. I said, "Please, let me go."

He worriedly looked around and put a finger to his lips, "Shhh, not so loud. The others will hear us." The other men were still huddled around the fire, oblivious to anything else. Cri continued, "I just wanted to talk. The others are always rude to me." Tears filled his eyes.

I felt sorry for him but also saw an opportunity to escape. I said, "I'm sorry to hear it, that's not very nice of them. Why are they so rude to you?"

Cri sobbed, "We used to have a sister. She lived with us and would take care of us all. Then I made a mistake and burnt our house down. We all escaped, but she never made it out." His tears fell freely, and he started moaning mournfully.

I found myself sharing his feelings of grief. I tried to distance myself and be practical, but my emotions were taking over. I asked, "What was her name?"

He snivelled, "Anna."

The name reverberated in my head, and it could've been shouted for the shock it gave me. Anna. My mother's name was Anna. The feeling of sadness intensified, and I sat numbly as tears rolled down my face.

Cri continued between sobs, "It wasn't my fault. It all happened so quickly. They all blame me and now no one will talk to me."

Cri looked exactly as I felt, all beaten down and ready to give up. Even his thoughts were mirroring my own. I had never realised before, but part of me blamed myself for my mom's death. She had died from cancer, but maybe there was something I could have done. My dad had never looked at me the same afterwards and had never tried to comfort me.

My mom had been diagnosed soon after I was born. Maybe he thought I was to blame? Was that why he stopped talking to me? I stared into the flame of the fire and felt the cold sink deeper. The heaviness in the air forced me to shrink further. Cri was mumbling to himself and had forgotten about me. He stumbled back to the fire.

My contemplative thoughts added to my feeling of hopelessness. I knew I needed to get out of here and back into the forest outside, but I couldn't have gotten myself to move even if I had wanted to. Even with feeling sad, I felt a comfortability with the feeling. Like an old friend that I hadn't seen for a while. I knew it wasn't good for me, but I couldn't help but indulge it anyway. I lay on the burnt floor, the smell of ash and smoke in the air, feeling like this was suddenly a representation of my life. All up in flames and no hope of restoration.

The Last Leaf

I touched the side of my face and winced at the pain, I could feel the bruise already forming and my right cheek was puffy. I was still in shock about what had happened. I had heard Leah scream and then I burst in on four men trying to carry her away. Without thinking, I had tried to stop them, but one of the men had moved so quickly, and the next thing I knew I was waking up on the forest floor. I blamed myself.

Leah wouldn't have run off if I hadn't upset her, and maybe then she wouldn't have run into her captors. I'd been wandering around the forest for the last hour and I still had no idea where they could be. My panic was fogging my mind and I couldn't think of a plan. I couldn't believe that Leah had been taken.

I stumbled through the forest, hoping that I would find some sign of where they had gone. I didn't know what I would do if I found them, but all my focus was on finding her. I would but every direction I looked appeared to be the same. Every tree mirrored hundreds like them and the ground was undisturbed by any signs of people. I would need to come up with the next step of the plan once I knew where they were hiding.

I just hoped that Leah was all right. I froze as I heard a twig snapping nearby. No further noise came, but I was certain I had heard something. My heart was beating rapidly, and my heart pounded as adrenaline coursed through my body. I remained frozen, but the lack of movement and my need to do something became too great. I shouted out, "Leah! Where are you?"

A frenzy overtook me, and I started sprinting through the forest. I had no destination in mind, but I was filled with energy and I needed to do something with it. I continued shouting after her and running. My legs burnt and my throat ached from yelling, I lost track of how far I'd gone, and gave one final shout as I stopped. I looked around in consternation and wondered what I was going to do. I gave a yelp as I felt a hand on my shoulder. I whirled around and saw Gai. He smiled apologetically, but he wore a worried frown.

Gai said, "Has something happened to Leah?"

In between gasps for breath I replied, "Four men took her. I tried to stop them, but they hit me on the head, and knocked me out. Please help, I've no idea where they've taken her." All dislike for the man was gone. Right now, I needed his help and he was my best chance at getting Leah back.

A thunderous look passed across Gai's face and I took a step back. He said, "They have gone too far this time. They know that they are not allowed to touch travellers, especially after their last time."

"Has this happened before? What happened last time?"

Gai started striding away, I quickly followed. He distractedly spoke, "They used to host travellers who came through, but they made a fire and burnt their home down. They were banished, but now they've come back, and they've been sneaking around the forest trying to get rid of me." Gai barked a laugh, "They think that getting rid of me will lift their ban. I'd like to see them try."

Gai was walking so fast, I had to jog to keep up with him. I was too out of breath to ask any further questions, so I focused on staying with him. Gai knew exactly where he was going and walked confidently through the forest. I didn't know how he could tell where we were for everything looked the same to me. I was wondering how far we would have to go when he held out a hand for me to stop and motioned to be quiet.

As I fell silent, I could hear the low rumble of voices nearby. I cautiously looked around a tree and stared in wonder at the devastation in front of me. A tree as large as the one we climbed yesterday was burnt black. The fire must have spread as well, because all the trees in sight were burnt. I noticed the large gaping hole in the trunk and saw the flickering of light inside. Gai muttered angrily about a fire.

I was thinking that we needed to plan a sneaky rescue mission, but Gai started striding confidently toward the tree. I hesitated for a second before following. I hoped he knew what he was doing because I was not a great fighter. My head throbbed at the thought of getting hit again. As we neared the entrance, Gai whispered to me, "Don't look at the fire. Just get Leah out of there and leave. I'll deal with the rest." I thought that was a great plan and I quickly agreed. Gai looked like a superhero as he strode toward the tree.

We walked into a trap.

As soon as we entered the ravaged opening, shouting came from all around and I saw ropes being thrown around Gai. I ducked out the way and tried to escape. Out of the corner of my eye I saw Leah lying on the floor and I immediately changed course towards her. The shouting had risen to screams, but I ignored them and focused on Leah. She was lying on her side and I noticed that her eyes were red from tears and fixed on the flame.

I felt my own gaze being pulled toward the fire, but I forced myself to stare at Leah. Something was definitely wrong. Her eyes were sunken, and her skin was ice cold. Dread filled my body, but then I noticed her shallow breathing and her eyes briefly flickered towards me before going back to the fire.

She was mumbling, "I'm sorry, mom. I didn't want you to die." Leah groaned and shook her head as if trying to rid herself of bad memories. She said, "I would take your place if I could. I've been so lonely without you." Tears streamed down her face.

"I am here, Leah," I comforted her, "You are not alone. Come with me. We need to get out of this place."

I tried to coax her, but she muttered incoherently and remained still. Ignoring my throbbing head and tired limbs, I heaved her off the ground and began carrying her out. The scene behind me was better than I could've expected. Gai stood face to face with one of the men, the others appearing to have fled. I heard him say, "Brennan, it's over. You've lost, and now it's time for you to leave." Gai kicked dirt into the flame. As it went out Leah immediately slackened and her head rolled back.

"Gai, help! Leah just passed out."

He turned to us in surprise, as if he'd forgotten we were here. The man, Brennan, quickly spoke, "She needs the fire, without it she will die. Feel her skin, she is cold to the touch, she needs to get warm." I looked at Leah and then back at Brennan. He seemed genuine, but I wasn't sure.

Gai spoke calmly, "Lino, she needs to get out of her. This place is what's making her sick, she needs to be taken back to the life of the forest outside, not stay here in this destruction. You need to leave now; it will already be influencing you."

I noticed that I was more tired than usual, and my mind was processing information slowly. I stared dumbly at them both, but I didn't move. My arms started shaking as I held the unconscious Leah. What if the fire was the only thing keeping her alive? Why did she feel so cold? Maybe it would give me more energy?

Brennan seemed to sense victory, "That's right. Stay here with us, we will fix her. You will also feel better once you see the flame. Gai wants to keep you in the dark, he doesn't want you to know how wonderful the fire could be."

Gai smiled sadly, "You don't want this, it's nothing but pain and death. You need to trust me, please leave now."

I wondered if Gai was trying to keep me away from some truth. What if Brennan was right, and I needed the fire? Maybe the fire was the secret to Gai's good looks and happiness. I could use some of that in my own life. My foggy thoughts kept me from thinking clearly and Leah's weight in my arms tempted me to lay her down. A bit of warmth would be good. Maybe they could start another fire.

"Lino, look at Leah. Does she look better off from being near the fire?"

The earnestness in Gai's eyes and Leah's unconscious body snapped me out of my stupor. I began stumbling toward the exit. I saw Brennan scream as he launched himself at Gai. They both went down, but I didn't see what happened next. I walked toward the green forest. I could feel the heaviness pulling me down and slowing my movements, Leah's weight seemed to increase. I was half-way there when my knees buckled, and I fell over. I tried to protect Leah as we tumbled down together. Lying on my back, I felt my eyelids closing on me. I tried to get up, but my body didn't respond.

My eyes slid shut.

$$\text{\Large ⸙ ⸙ ⸙}$$

I felt powerful arms pick me up, and I was laid carefully on the ground. I heard whispering next to me and then a groggy groan. A presence knelt down next to me and said, "Lino, you need to wake up. Feel the ground giving you energy, fight against the tiredness."

I focused on the ground beneath me and I could feel the energy pulsing through the forest. I concentrated on the strength around me and forced my eyes open. I was looking up into the face of a grinning Gai. As soon as my eyes were open, the rest of my body came awake. Gai helped me to my feet. It relieved me to see that Leah was already standing, looking sheepish. I gave her a goofy grin and she smiled back.

Something had changed in her eyes though; the innocence and naivety was gone. I wasn't sure what had happened to her in that place, but it had taken something from her. Or had it given something? As if she knew of the terrible things in the world, and yet still decided to continue. I wasn't sure if it was a good thing or not.

I looked at Gai and asked, "What happened?"

Gai explained, "It's a place of death, anyone who spends too much time there, loses their will to live. Fire has been banned from this forest for a reason, any who gazes at the flame feels their joy being sapped from them. Instead of warming you, it takes all the warmth from your soul. It's a dangerous place." He looked worriedly at Leah, but then continued, "The men there all fell into the trap and now they are forever cold. They can get better, but they need to leave the fire behind."

Leah said, "Cri said that his sister had died in that place and that it was his fault. He had started the fire that burnt down the tree."

Gai said gently, "That was a lie. They were attempting to draw you further into their sadness." He hesitated but then asked, "Did they mention someone you lost?"

Her response was just above a whisper, "Anna. Their sister had the same name as my mom."

"Grief is a powerful feeling and can last for years. Sometimes it never goes away." Gai looked at Leah and then to me. I saw the sadness in his eyes and wondered who he had lost.

I asked, "Why would they stay there?"

A sad look passed over Gai's face, "Because they've become addicted to the feeling, although it's killing them, and the longer they stare at the fire, the harder it is to leave it behind." He looked me in the eye, "Make sure you don't get caught in the trap. Being sad is okay, but you need to be brave enough to let it go as well."

I wondered what he meant, but I saw Leah slowly nod her head as if she understood. I was completely lost, but I decided not to pry and ask questions. It looked like it was something that neither Leah nor Gai wanted to speak about. Gai seemed to snap himself out of his reverie, his usual energy returned, "Let's get you out of here. It's time for you to leave Arbre and get to the Prince."

Devon Hoole

Family

Gai led us through the forest as we walked in silence. An awkward air hung between us, and I ignored it in the hope that it would disappear on its own. The trees got smaller and began thinning out as we continued. I noticed that under the leaves, sand patches were beginning to appear.

All my strength had returned, and I saw that Leah was also looking better. She no longer looked so tired. I tried to catch her eye, but she was focused on her feet and seemed lost in thought. I wanted some time to talk to her in private. We needed to clear the air and reconnect. I didn't like how we had left it, and since then, I hadn't had a chance to talk to her properly.

The Last Leaf

I hoped that as soon as we left the forest, it would just be the two of us again and then we can chat. I hoped Gai wouldn't decide to come with us. Although I appreciated his help rescuing Leah, I didn't want him around all the time.

Gai told us he was going to go on ahead to scout the area, and we must just continue heading straight. He gave me a wink and then jogged on ahead and left Leah and I alone. I cleared my throat, "How are you feeling?"

Leah shrugged with her voice expressionless as she spoke, "I'm fine."

"I'm glad," I tried to sound upbeat. I gently touched her elbow, and she stopped. I blurted, "I'm sorry for what I said. I was angry, I didn't mean any of it. Please, please forgive me. I hate myself for what happened, and I wish I could take it all back."

Leah still hadn't looked me in the eye, but she said, "Lino, it's just…"

I never got to hear what she was going to say, because Gai suddenly shouted. He was calling us to move quickly. I worriedly looked around, but I didn't see anyone chasing us. We ran towards his voice.

We cleared the forest and were suddenly standing at the beginning of an enormous desert. I groaned as I saw all the sand and nothing else. I hoped this would not be our next part of the journey. I wasn't too keen to get stuck in a desert. Gai was motioning for us to come towards him, he spoke quickly, "You see that group up ahead, on the horizon." I squinted my eyes, and I saw the group he spoke of. It seemed about four or five people.

Gai continued, "You need to catch up to them as quickly as possible. It's not wise to travel alone and I don't know when the next group could leave. You need to catch them." It all happened so quickly, Gai hugged Leah and whispered something into her ear, her eyes filled with tears, but she smiled back at him and nodded. I wondered what that was about.

He enveloped me in a hug and said, "Remember what I said about grief and sadness. Look after each other." He pushed me along. We broke into a run towards the group ahead of us. I watched Leah run and wondered if Gai had been warning me of something. I shook my head. I needed to get out of this place.

I tried to catch up with Leah, but all her energy seemed to have returned and she was running as fast as she could. Despite the distance from the group, we caught up to them quickly. The group noticed us coming and stopped to watch our approach. Leah had pulled ahead and had finished with greetings by the time I arrived.

There were five of them, I was sure it was a family as they all had the same squished faces. The mother had a hardness to her look that I didn't like, and the father had shifty eyes. Two big boys were there, and they had the same look as their mother. A small girl stood behind her mother's skirt as she shyly watched us. All of them wore tanned clothing that covered all their skin, they looked tired and dusty. I guessed that would happen to you in the desert.

Despite their appearance they had greeted Leah warmly, and she smiled gratefully at their hospitality. I approached, and I was certain I saw a look of annoyance flash across the mother's face, but a smile quickly replaced it, "Welcome weary traveller. I'm Rebecca, and this little angel behind me is Zilla." Zilla buried her face in her mom's skirt.

The three men shook my hand, and I flinched at their firm grips. The two boys named themselves as Dugal and Huxley, and the father introduced himself as Phobus. They offered us a drink of water and we gratefully accepted. I looked around at the expanse of desert and back at Arbre. The forest was already small in the distance. I was surprised how fast we had travelled.

Leah asked, "Do you mind if we travel with you? We've just come from Arbre and Gai told us that it's better to travel in a group."

Rebecca squealed in delight and hugged Leah. She said, "Of course you can travel with us. It would be our pleasure. Wouldn't it, Phobus?" The father grunted in agreement. The two brothers watched me, and I smiled at them, neither smiled in return. I looked away and focused on the sand.

The mother, Rebecca, spoke, "If you don't mind, we would like to travel a bit further before we stop. There's a place up ahead where it's a good spot to rest for the night."

And so, with our small new family, we continued walking. I looked back at the forest and felt a sense of loss. I had a feeling that I was leaving the last bit of familiarity. Rebecca had her arm around Leah's shoulders, and they were happily talking. I was glad to see Leah looking more relaxed. I quietly walked at the back of the group.

It looked exactly as I guessed a desert would look like, all I could see was sand, not a rock or a tree in sight. I looked down at the brown sand and felt the grains already in my sandals. I was surprised the sand wasn't hot, and I quickly took off my sandals to walk barefoot. It was soft and comfortable on my feet as I happily continued walking behind the family.

We reached our resting place for the night as dusk was setting in. It looked the same as everything else, I could see no reason why this was the best spot. Dugal and Huxley were sent to fetch some wood, and I realised the barren looking trees were probably a helpful landmark. Rebecca, Zilla and Leah began digging a small hole as a kettle and pot were brought out.

Unsure of what to do, I took a seat nearby and watched all the activity. The boys came back with wood and made a fire. Water from a flask was poured into the kettle and vegetables and meat was thrown into the pot for a stew.

It was the first time I had seen meat since being here and my mouth watered. We had been living on vegetables and fruit for the last few days.

The father, Phobus, was entertaining little Zilla by drawing pictures in the sand. She sat in his lap, suggesting new ideas. I noticed that he was an excellent artist; even with a stick in the sand, you could clearly tell what he was making. He was now drawing a herd of horses and I stared in awe as they seemed to move. He then wiped it clean and started drawing large sea creatures, some I recognised, others I didn't.

I was lost in wonder at the sight of the pictures, when I heard Rebecca call everyone for dinner. Leah came over to me with a bowl that I gratefully took it and tucked in. I hoped she would sit with me, but she went back to Rebecca and they continued chatting. How could they have so much to talk about?

The food was amazing though, the meat mixed with the vegetables really hit the spot and I enjoyed the feeling of a full stomach. We all finished and thanked the cooks for the wonderful meal. Rebecca gave all the credit to Leah and her face flushed in happiness. Next the call for music started and I was surprised to see the two boys were musicians. One had a wonderfully carved flute shaped instrument and the other had a small guitar.

I watched in wonder as they began playing. The music that filled the air was mesmerizing, the sound reaching into my being and seeming to harmonize with my soul.

Phobus and Rebecca stood up and began to dance with each other. I was transfixed by the sight, they moved as one and were perfectly in time with the music. I braved a glance over at Leah and was relieved to see she was also absorbed in the show, I didn't want to have to dance as well. It was something I feared and always avoided if possible. I quickly looked away as Leah glanced at me.

The dancing couple were moving quickly. Three swift steps and then they slowed down and stretched out the music. Every movement accentuated the rhythm. Then they burst with movement again. The tone of the music changed, and a voice filled the air and I was surprised to see little Zilla singing. She said no words, but her voice became the melody of the music. I closed my eyes and enjoyed the magical performance. I fell asleep to the sound of music and laughter.

⸭ ⸭ ⸭

I awoke with a start. I looked around and saw that everyone had curled up on the floor asleep. No tents or blankets were needed as the temperature was moderate enough. I wondered what the time was as light was still in the air. It looked the same as the night before and I wondered if it had gotten any darker since then. The light seemed to be staying around the further we travelled.

Leah had Zilla curled up beside her and the boys were sleeping a respectful distance from her. I noticed that I was on the opposite side of the fire from the family. I was hurt that Leah was with them, but I shook my head annoyedly, I had fallen asleep early. They probably didn't want to disturb me and if they asked Leah to stay by them how could she say no. No one else seemed to be waking up, so I decided to sleep a bit more. My eyes slid shut.

It didn't last long though and I awoke with a start again. Sleeping outside was a weird experience and I still wasn't used to it. I felt like I always had to be on guard and aware of my surroundings. This time when I looked up, I saw Phobus and the two boys moving around. They walked off towards the few barren trees, I guessed they were getting some more wood. I decided to go help.

I needed to try and become more friendly with them, who knows how long we will be together, and the journey will be a lot more pleasant if we all got along. They saw me coming and watched my approach. I felt exposed under their gazes, but I attempted to be upbeat, greeting them and getting a nod in return.

I asked, "Do you need any help?"

Phobus shared a look with his sons and then shrugged, "Sure."

I was directed to pick up little sticks, while Dugal and Huxley started breaking branches off the trees. "So how long have you been journeying for?" I asked.

Huxley answered as a branch cracked in his hands, "About a week or two, it's been so boring I've lost track of time."

Dugal spoke, "We were with another group, but we had to separate. They went ahead of us." Huxley gave him a sharp look and he stopped talking.

I wondered what that was about, but I asked instead, "Have you seen a guy named Clay, he looks like me, but just a bit older?"

They both shook their heads, and I believed them. It seemed they were the first people who hadn't seen Clay. I inwardly sighed and wondered how I was ever going to catch up to him.

I was surprised when Phobus asked, "How long have you known Leah for?"

I felt a tension in the air, and everything seemed to have quietened in wait for my response, I said, "We've been neighbours all our lives, so we practically grew up with one another."

He asked again, "It seems like she's a bit upset with you. What happened there?"

The question felt intrusive and I wondered why he cared, but I answered anyway, "We had a fight yesterday and I said some hurtful things." I didn't like the gleam that shone in Phobus's eyes as I spoke. I quickly added, "But we're fine now. We sorted it out." The shine dimmed from his eyes. I tried to get the topic off of Leah, "How much longer do you think we'll be in the desert for?"

Any desire to talk to me seemed to have left them, they shrugged and grumbled a vague response. I decided I needed to talk to Leah and see what she was thinking, I didn't have a good feeling about these people. We finished collecting the wood and headed back. No further conversation happened, and I kept catching Dugal glancing at me.

The rest of the family and Leah were already awake. The fire was lit, and I was left on the outskirts as the men chatted amongst themselves. Last night I was initially worried about the fire, but I realised it was just a normal fire. The strange draining of the flames must only happen in the forest.

The man in the green suit had warned us about fires and not starting them. It occurred to me that we hadn't seen the man for the desert yet. I wondered when we would see the man in the camel coloured suit. So far, we hadn't been given any instructions.

I smiled as Leah came and sat down next to me. I quietly asked, "How are you feeling?"

"I'm feeling good. It's nice to be out in the open, really feels like my mind is clearing up. The fresh air is nice." She took a deep breath and sighed.

I noticed she still hadn't looked at me, I heard the pleading in my voice, but I couldn't help it, "I'm really sorry about what I said. I'm glad you are here with me. I was just being stupid and wasn't thinking."

Leah looked at me for the first time, I could still see the change in her eyes, but now they had softened, "It's alright. Considering everything else that happened, I think that was minor compared to the rest."

We both chuckled. I could feel the wall between us lowering. I wanted to ask what happened when she was taken, but I didn't want to push her. I still felt like I was on precarious ground and I didn't want to make another mistake. I watched Rebecca and Zilla walk towards the men and join their conversation. I voiced my suspicions, "What do you think of our travelling family? Something seems a bit strange about them."

Leah shrugged, and began smoothing out the sand, "I like them."

"I don't know, I just get a weird feeling about them." I realised that I had been wrong about Gai, and maybe I shouldn't be so quick to judge. I tried to be supportive, "Well, they seem to like you."

Immediately, I knew I had said something wrong. Leah froze and her eyes burned, she hissed softly, "They must be crazy if they like me then?"

"No, Leah, I didn't mean that..."

But she got up and stalked away. Rebecca noticed her going, gave a small smirk in my direction, and then followed. She put her arm around Leah as they walked. I watched them go and knew that I had messed up again, but this time it really had been a misunderstanding. I was glad that the family liked her, it was good for her. Especially since we were struggling to get along, it was nice for her to have others to talk to and feel part of their group.

Now I realised that I shouldn't have said anything about them and left my suspicions alone. I had just wanted to protect her, but it always seemed to backfire. I needed to give her some space and allow time to heal the wounds caused. I looked around me and saw Dugal watching me again, he quickly looked away as our eyes met. I chose to ignore it and try my best to get along with everyone.

Leah and Rebecca were gone for a long time, and Phobus started getting annoyed by the delay. He kept shooting accusing looks at me and then would mumble under his breath. Everything was packed and waiting to go by the time they returned. Leah's eyes were red, and her cheeks were flushed. Rebecca still had an arm around her, and she gave me the same accusing look as her husband. As if protecting Leah from me, she guided her to the rest of the family.

I heard sympathetic words and awkward patting on the back from the boys. Zilla took Leah's hand and smiled up at her. With that, they collected their things and started off. I offered to carry something, but I was ignored and given a stern look that told me to keep my distance. I was left to walk behind them.

The next few days were tough, but I ignored it out of respect for Leah and keeping her happy. She was happy here and Rebecca had practically adopted her as a daughter. Leah was thriving and loved the attention. I understood why, and even though I thought the attention was strange, I accepted it. I would not be stupid enough to bring it up again. We had barely spoken to one another and only shared polite words of greeting. We were drifting further apart.

The rest of the family had taken Leah's side, and they made it clear that I was only being tolerated because of her. I walked alone; I sat by myself and ate alone. I slept at a distance from them and didn't join in with any of the nightly music rituals. Despite the isolation, I kept reminding myself how happy Leah was and that I owed her this, so I put up with the disapproving looks and sometimes rude remarks on my behalf.

The time alone gave me time to think, and I had been thinking a lot about our journey so far and how strange it had been. We had been met on a hilltop by four men in suits and sandals, and each one told us something that was forbidden as we entered their land. I had overheard Phobus reminding Zilla that the man in the camel coloured suit had said to keep moving. That explained why Leah and I hadn't seen him.

I brought my thoughts back to my reminiscing. First, the path had been terrible to walk on, but we had been told to stay on it, Leah hadn't listened and then got stuck. We made it to Bijou with all of its jewels and fancy living. I had fallen into the trap and only wrestling the giant, and taking off that pendant, had helped me break free from the spell. Then I had made the mistake of drinking the golden drink, Miel, and only Leah tricking me about Clay had drawn me away from that. Then the giant tree and talking to the eagle, Absaar. Kissing Leah on the platform on top of the world and feeling like everything was going to be alright. Then meeting Gai and immediately being jealous. Hurting Leah and her getting captured, then having Gai rescue us both. Now we were wondering the desert with no end in sight and no idea of what's next.

All the while I had learnt nothing about Clay and where he was, and my suspicion of the Prince had grown with every passing day. Nothing about this place had been good so far and I felt a bone-weary tiredness about it all. I wasn't sure how much more I could take. I felt an ache at the thought of Clay, I realised that I hadn't thought about him often enough and I felt guilty for allowing myself to get distracted.

The whole reason I was here was to get him back, but I had made no progress at all. The pace we were moving was too slow and I was feeling itchy with frustration. Since we had been to three of the four environments, I assumed that the ocean place would be next, so I kept listening for the sound of water. I wondered what would have happened if we had chosen the sea village first. Would that have allowed us to avoid all this? I tried not to dwell on those thoughts and convinced myself that we probably would have had to go through it all anyway.

On the third day of walking in the desert, we came to a small oasis where we could refill our water canisters. I marvelled at the sudden greenery of life that was surrounded by dry desert. Beautifully lush trees and green grass filled the small area. My heart sank as I heard Phobus saying that they would spend a few days here. I tried to argue that we needed to listen to the man in the suit and keep moving, but I was ignored. I wondered how long we could stay in the same place before something went wrong. I just imagined the oasis sinking and disappearing into oblivion.

I pulled Leah aside and tried to convince her, "We need to keep moving, you know what happens when we don't listen to the men in the suits."

Leah opened her mouth to protest, but I quickly spoke again, "I'm not throwing anything in your face, I'm just pointing out what we've experienced. I need to find Clay; I can't wait around anymore. I feel like time is running out. We only have the ocean village left and then I assume we'll get to the Prince's city. I need to keep going."

At the mention of Clay, Leah's eyes softened, she said slowly, "I know it's been slow going, but this is our only option at the moment. We need to stay with Rebecca."

I had been thinking of another option and now I brought it up, "Dugal mentioned that they separated from another family and that they went on ahead. I think if we push for a day, we could catch up with them."

"I don't think Rebecca and Phobus will be keen to do that. They were hurt by the other group and they are tired from walking for so long. They have been doing this for a lot longer than we have."

I realised I had made up my mind and I wanted to leave, "Then let's go, just the two of us." I took her hands in mine, "I'm going to go, please come with me."

Hope soared in my heart as I saw her considering it, but just as fast as it had risen it was crushed, she said, "I'm sorry Lino, I can't go."

"Please Leah, don't say that. Just come with me. Let's go."

She pulled her hands away from me, "I just can't".

I couldn't understand how she could choose these strange people over me. I looked over and saw Rebecca watching us out of the corner of her eye. The whole family seemed to be watching us. I lowered my voice in one last desperate attempt, "Something's not right about them, you need to trust me on this. I don't know what it is, but I keep feeling that they are trying to keep us apart and push me away." I saw Rebecca come towards us and my heart sank as I realised, I was losing Leah. She put her arm around Leah and snarled at me.

I was so angry that Leah couldn't see what I could, I stared at Rebecca and said, "We need to keep moving, we were told not to stay in the same place for too long. Spending a couple of days here will not end well." I looked desperately at Leah, "Come with me. Let's go."

Rebecca barked a cold laugh, "Go with you, why would she do that? She's happy here with us. But we do think it's time for you to leave." She shoved a flask of water into my hands, "Leah's going to be traveling with us to the Prince."

I felt breathless, Leah wasn't looking at me, but I knew I wouldn't be able to change her mind. The rest of the family stood with their arms crossed and blank faced. I realised I had no choice but to leave. I tried hardening my heart, but this was a pain I couldn't ignore.

Without another word, I turned and left.

I walked numbly, unbelieving of what had just happened. Leah had chosen them over me. I was trying to convince myself that somehow they had tricked her into staying, and that soon I would hear her running after me, but I knew that this wasn't the truth. I wondered if I had done the right thing in leaving. It felt wrong not having Leah by my side.

I considered going back, but it was clear that Rebecca and the family did not want me there anymore, so I kept walking. I tried to convince myself that I was doing this for Clay, and that everything would be alright once I found him. We would go home, and Leah would find her own way back with her new family. I was sad, but I tried not to let myself dwell on it. I needed to harden my heart and carry on. This was what I wanted when I first got here, to do this journey alone. I guess I got my wish.

I looked back one last time and waited for a few minutes. This would be my final wait, and then I needed to pick up the pace. I sighed as I saw no sign of Leah. It was time to go. I stiffened my spine and started jogging in the direction that felt right. There was no path or any indication of where to go, but I felt pulled in this direction and I trusted my instinct. Either I would catch up with the group before me, or I would make it to the next part of the journey. Either way, I wasn't going to worry myself with who I'd left behind.

Time stretched on and I focused on putting one foot in front of another. I would jog for as long as I could, then walk for a while and repeat. The exercise was good for my mind, everything was blank, and I just had to worry about moving forward. I didn't have to think about anyone else's feelings or worry that I was not being good company. I could just relax and be myself.

I felt the same way when Clay and I were together, family knows everything about you so there's no point in pretending. It was a feeling that I treasured. I had started feeling the same with Leah, but it hadn't lasted, and now I needed to regroup and get back to real family. I missed my parents, even uncle Telly, and I realised I had taken their presence for granted.

I missed a step as I saw dots on the horizon. I squinted and realised that it was the other group. I used the last of my energy to jog the last stretch. There were only three of them, a man, a woman, and a young girl. The young girl had spotted me and waved happily. Her parents stopped and waved as well. I was relieved to see welcoming smiles. They had kind faces and I immediately liked them. I stopped running a short distance away and walked the last bit. I called out a greeting.

As I got to them, the man shook my hand and introduced himself, "Welcome, I'm Abiel and this is my wife Avery, and our daughter, Fay. Please take a seat, you look exhausted." He pulled out a small fold out chair and I gratefully took a seat. Abiel was well-built and probably in his mid-thirties, a few days of scruff was on his face, but instead of making him look unkempt, it suited him.

His wife, Avery, was wearing a loose dress, if fairies existed, I guessed they would look like her, she was slim and had a humorous twinkle in her eyes. Fay was practically a small version of her mother, she stuck out her hand and my heart melted as I shook it.

I realised I had been staring and hadn't said anything, "Sorry, I'm a bit out of breath."

Avery offered me a drink of water and I gratefully took it, she said, "How long have you been walking Audun for?"

I frowned and said, "Audun? What's that?"

Avery's laughed chimed and she spread her arms, "This is Audun. All the sand around us. Didn't the man in the suit tell you?"

"I haven't seen him yet. Maybe he knows that you'll tell me." Not wanting more questions, I quickly added, "You wanted to know how long I've been walking?" I decided to keep Leah and the other family to myself, I said, "Just a few days. I heard a group had left before me and so I've been trying to catch up to you."

Abiel and Avery shared a look. Abiel asked, "Do you only have a flask? No bag or anything?"

I tensed, but tried to shrug nonchalantly, "I found this flask when I left the forest, all I have are the clothes on my back."

Avery's face softened, she patted me on the shoulder. Her sudden kindness and motherly touch brought tears to my eyes. Embarrassed, I looked away and hid my face by taking another sip of water. I wasn't sure why I suddenly felt so emotional, I decided I must be more tired than I thought, or there was still something in the air that was affecting me.

I let out a shaky breath and said, "Thank you, I really appreciate your kindness. It's been a tough journey and the last few days have been hard. Sorry about this." I wiped my nose and looked over at them, they all sat cross legged on the floor.

Abiel waved my apology away, "No worries, it must be tough traveling alone. I know I would struggle without these two." He lovingly looked at his small family.

My heart ached at the thought of Leah and losing her. I looked away again.

Abiel said, "You mentioned the forest, did you travel through there as well?"

Without thinking, I began explaining my entire journey, from arriving on the hilltop until walking into their lives now. The more I spoke I felt a weight lift off my chest and I wouldn't have been able to stop even if I had wanted to. I edited my story slightly to keep Leah out of it, but it felt good to talk to people about all this. It was a relief to express all the thoughts that had been swirling around in my head for so long.

The small family watched me with interest, and they were a great audience. They looked anxious when I told the tough parts and smiled happily when it turned out well. I enjoyed talking and not being interrupted, I wasn't used to it. I finished the story off and they all clapped.

Avery shook her head in wonder, "What a journey! You've really had an eventful time."

Little Fay asked, "You've had no one with you? You must have been so lonely." She gave me a hug.

I felt guilty about lying to them, but I couldn't bring myself to tell them about Leah. I patted Fay's small shoulder and hated myself for the deception.

"How about some tea?" Abiel grinned.

Fay and Avery cheered, I couldn't help but smile and agree that some tea would be nice. Despite being in the desert and having run for the past few hours, I realised that the temperature was still pleasant. I wanted to continue moving, but I tried to stand, and my legs refused to budge. A small break and some tea would be welcomed. I enjoyed the easy natured chatter among the family. It was in sharp contrast with the group I had just abandoned and instead of feeling left out, I felt included in the family immediately.

After tea and a piece of cake each, we decided to carry on walking. I managed to get to my feet, and we all laughed as I took my first few rubbery steps, but each step got stronger and I was soon walking normally again. We moved at a comfortable pace, with Fay constantly weaving around us, she was full of energy. Despite being happy that I found Abiel and Avery, and traveling with them, I couldn't help but feel a deep sadness that Leah wasn't here with me.

Abiel noticed my look and whispered to me, "I know it's none of my business, but if you're running from something, maybe it would be better if you faced it instead."

I felt relief that he had spoken, but I shook my head, "It's too late. I can't go back now."

Abiel said, "There's always a way, even if we think it's a lost cause. We need to fight for those we love."

"But what if I'm torn between two people I love? One is ahead of me and the other is behind. Clay is my brother and I need to find him. He is my priority right now. Anything else becomes a distraction." I slide my feet along the sand, the grains sprinkled over my bare feet.

"If you're making the right decision, why is it still bothering you?" Abiel raised an eyebrow.

I looked back towards Leah and said, "I don't know. I guess I wish I never had to make the decision in the first place."

Abiel nodded his head thoughtfully. We fell silent and walked companionly alongside each other. I continued to battle with the tension inside me. Something didn't feel right about leaving Leah, but what other choice did I have? She chose them over me. Clay could be needing me. I needed to remember why I was here.

Rebecca had said they'd take Leah home, she was probably safer with them. I remembered what Gai had told me as we left the forest, he had said that grief was normal, but I also needed to be brave enough to let it go. I wondered if he had been talking about Leah. Had he known we would go our separate ways? My heart ached with a sense of loss at every step I took towards Clay.

☙ ☙ ☙

I helped set up a fire with Abiel at the spot we were spending the night. No sign of life except for us. I was tired of only seeing sand. The day was dimming, but some light stubbornly clung in the air. I asked, "Do you know why it doesn't get fully dark anymore?"

Little Fay danced around us and eagerly answered, "That's because the Prince is close. Isn't that right, dad?" A swirl of sand suddenly danced in the distance.

Abiel laughed and stroked Fay's hair, "That's right." He looked at me and said, "We've been told that it never gets dark in the Prince's city." Another swirl of sand disappeared in the distance.

I dubiously looked around and asked, "Why does something always happen when someone mentions him?"

Avery laughed and said, "Because everything here is his. His creation acknowledges its creator." Avery and Fay started dancing and singing, "The Prince". They danced among swirls of sand that appeared to move with them. I was transfixed. What was this place? And what kind of man could get the world reacted in this way?

Abiel clapped me on the back and said, "Amazing, isn't it?"

I wasn't sure what it was, but it terrified me. In the dimmed light, it looked like giant tornadoes consuming the mother and daughter. Clay was going to this man? What could I do? Suddenly, I feared what would happen if I didn't succeed.

Abiel saw my look and asked, "What's wrong? They aren't in any danger. Look, the sand isn't even touching them."

I was shocked to see that Avery and Fay returned without being brushed by any sand. I shook my head and got to my feet. I said, "I need to go. I must get to my brother. I've wasted too much time already." I searched for my water flask.

"What about the one you left behind?"

I dropped all pretences, "She chose Rebecca over me. I tried to convince her, but she wouldn't come with me. Now, I need to get to my brother before I lose him. I can wait for Leah at the city. I'm sure I can stop her too."

Abiel had frozen and I saw that both Avery and Fay's faces had paled. Avery asked, "Did you say Rebecca? Is her husband Phobus? And they have two sons?"

I nodded, "They also have a daughter, they were the group I was with before coming to find you." I suddenly remembered that Abiel and Avery were the ones who had separated from them. I said, "Sorry for lying to you. I just wanted to forget what happened." I couldn't find my flask. Maybe I should leave it.

Abiel said urgently, "Lino, they don't have a daughter. It's only the four of them, their little girl died a long time ago."

My head felt like it was suddenly full of wool. I couldn't believe what I was hearing. I stammered, "Of course they have a daughter. I saw her. I listened to her sing every night."

Avery continued speaking, "They tried to steal Fay from us. Rebecca is obsessed with replacing her daughter."

She walked up to me and spoke urgently, "You need to get your friend back. They are abusive, terrible people. They lure young women to them and then use them as slaves. They come between families and drive the loved ones away. They tried it with us, but there was no way we would ever leave Fay. Once we realised what they were up to, we snuck away one night."

My heart was thumping in my chest and I struggled to process what they were saying. All I knew was that I had made another mistake and that I needed to get Leah back. But what about Clay? I would be going in the wrong direction. He could be in more danger.

Abiel took a small bag out of his rucksack and put a few supplies in it. He handed it to me and said, "You need to get her back."

I hesitated a moment before making my decision. I thanked them, slung the bag over my back and started running. I just wished Leah was all right and nothing would happen to her. I was consumed with thoughts of Clay and Leah as I ran. I hoped I was making the right decision.

I ran with everything that I had.

⁂

Nothing had felt the same since Lino had left. I had

watched him walk away and my heart broke, I couldn't believe what had just happened. I felt the urge to chase after him, but Rebecca's strong arm was still wrapped around my shoulders. She had sighed as if Lino's presence had been a weight on her shoulders, she turned to me and smiled.

It was the first time that I saw something else behind those eyes, there was a look of triumph and she grinned at her husband. I tried to move away but she held me tighter, she was still looking at her husband as she said, "We've been waiting so long Phobus, now we've finally been sent someone to help us."

Phobus came and wrapped Rebecca in a tight hug, I heard him say, "Our dear little Zilla has sent someone to replace her."

Shocked, I looked around and realised that Zilla was nowhere to be seen. I strained my eyes searching for her among some of the greenery, but I had a sinking feeling she was not here. Rebecca had let go of me in the hug and I slowly began moving backwards. I suddenly felt extremely vulnerable by myself with this family.

I was still struggling to process what was going on, but the voice inside me was telling me to run. I spun around, but was met by Dugal and Huxley, who were blocking my way. I froze when I heard Rebecca speak, "Leah, what's wrong?"

I looked over at her, and the genuine concern in her face made me pause, "Where's Zilla? What's going on?"

Rebecca made soothing gestures, "She chose you!" A happy smile played on her lips, "She wants you to stay with us."

Phobus continued, "We were so sad when we lost her, and we have been wandering this desert feeling lost and without hope. Then you came and we knew that you were the one. When you spoke of Zilla and heard her singing every night, we knew for certain that you were meant to be with us. Your friend was the only thing in the way of that, but now that he's gone, you can stay with us."

Huxley had an eager look on his face, but I noticed that Dugal was struggling to look me in the eye. In the end, the concern on Rebecca's face made me relax and I allowed myself to breathe again. I nodded and she let out a yelp of celebration.

"Let's have some tea in celebration." Rebecca looked expectantly at me, "Will you do us the honours?"

Eager to please my new adopted family, I started the fire and began heating some tea. I wondered how Lino was doing; I hoped he was safe and that he would find Clay soon. We had been through so much together I felt part of me was missing now that he wasn't around. I understood why he left, I'd been terrible to him and I'd pushed him away.

Him walking way was still fresh in my mind, but I couldn't remember why I hadn't gone with him. I looked over at Rebecca. Like before, I felt that powerful connection with her. Something about her reminded me of my mother and I felt this need to be with her. The desire to be around her increased, but I wasn't getting the feeling I was after, something was still missing, and I hoped that the longer we were together the sooner that feeling would be satisfied.

I poured the tea and carried it over, I so desperately wanted this to be my new home. I needed them to like me, and I was willing to do what it takes to remain part of the family.

҂ ҂ ҂

I ran, and I ran. Nothing would stop me. I needed to get to Leah. The light was hanging in its frozen dimness, and I realised that I had practically been running an entire day. Once away and now back, but this time I was fuelled by my desire to be back with Leah. I didn't know what I would do once I got there, but I knew for certain I wasn't leaving without her again.

I slowed to a jog as I saw the oasis. Luckily, they had chosen a place among the trees and so I had some protection as I neared. I heard the chatter of people and the occasional bark of laughter. Knowing they wouldn't allow Leah to walk away with me, I hid away until they fell asleep. Or try to find a way to get her by herself. The laughter came again; I wondered if Leah would want to leave with me. What if she still refused? I shook my head. She would come. Even if I had to carry her away kicking and screaming.

I dared to go as close as I could. I found a small clump of bushes and crawled on my belly towards it. The scene before me looked familiar, but now I saw it with new eyes. Instead of Leah happily helping with dinner, I saw her as a lost soul being taken advantage of. I let out a sigh of relief that she looked fine; I hadn't thought they would hurt her, but I had still worried.

I looked closer, and I realised she was crying. No one else seemed to notice or care, as they carried on with their conversation. I fought down the urge to storm in there and get her out immediately. I looked over at Huxley and Phobus, and I knew that I would never get passed them.

I froze. Where was Dugal? He wasn't with the rest. I slowly began crawling backwards. I reached the nearest tress and strong hands grabbed the back of my shirt and I was yanked to my feet. I wanted to shout out, but I stopped myself as I saw the look on Dugal's face. He worriedly looked back over my shoulder in the direction of his family.

He whispered, "Don't say anything. Come with me." He let go and started walking away. Totally confused, but also intrigued, I followed. He led me to the outskirts of the oasis and then turned to me. He seemed to be thinking of what to say and fighting an internal battle. He finally spoke, "You shouldn't be here. You shouldn't have come back." He ran his hand through his hair.

I felt my anger bristle, "I've come to get Leah, and I'm not leaving without her. Abiel and Avery told me what you guys are up too. There's no way Leah's becoming your slave."

Dugal flinched as if slapped, "No need to shout. Do you want everyone to know you're here? Trust me, they won't be as welcoming as me." He held up a hand to stop me from talking again, "Let me talk for a bit."

I begrudgingly nodded.

Dugal took a deep breath, it seemed like he had made up his mind about something, "Look, we aren't as bad as you think. Yes, I know this is bad, and my mother took it too far. It didn't start out like this, we've just been in this desert for so long, wondering aimlessly. It changes something in you. I can't even remember how long ago we lost Zilla," tears sprang into his eyes, "We don't know what happened. She was fine one day and then the next she got a fever and was dead within a few hours. We had just been to a festival that the Prince had come through, and Zilla was even lucky enough to be touched by him. He picked her out in the crowd and kissed her hand. Next day she was dead."

"Do you think the Prince did something to her?" The trees around us rustled at the mention of the Prince. I flinched at the noise.

Dugal shrugged and wiped his nose, "I don't know. When you saw how he looked at her, you wouldn't think it possible, he had the kindest eyes I had ever seen. But now I'm not sure. There's no other explanation. Anyway, now my mom is convinced that if we leave the desert then we will lose Zilla forever. She's convinced that Zilla is still here in some way and that maybe we will come back to us if we wait long enough."

"Then why do you need Leah; she can't bring your sister back. I'm sorry about your sister, but this makes no sense."

Dugal squeezed his eyes shut, "I know, why do you think I'm here talking to you and not calling the rest of my family. It started a while back when we met another group of travellers. They had a young girl who reminded us so much of Zilla, that we began to think that maybe it was her.

Soon we realised it wasn't, but something had snapped in my mom and she was convinced that if we could keep a girl with us, then maybe Zilla will be able to take her place. Don't ask me how she thought that would happen, but she's become desperate. When we tried to take Avery and Abiel's little girl, I knew that we were doing a terrible thing, but I didn't do anything to try stop it. Then you and Leah came."

A look of wonder came across his eyes, "Leah looks just like an older version of Zilla, even her mannerisms are similar. We were all so shocked and I tried talking my mom out of it. Telling her that Leah was too old, but she wouldn't hear any of it.

She saw an opportunity to pull you two apart and she made sure we treated you as an outcast, all the while she whispered lies into Leah's ears. My mom has a way with young women, they seem to sense her desire for a daughter, and it can be very tempting for some. Leah fit the bill perfectly." Dugal fell silent.

I heard the desperation in my voice, "Please help me, I need to get her out of here."

Dugal looked me dead in the eye. He seemed to be weighing me up, and then he made a decision, "Wait here, I'm going to send her to fetch water and then it's up to you to convince her. That's all I'll do." Without waiting for a response, he marched off.

I wrung my hands nervously as I waited. A few minutes passed and I heard someone approaching. I quickly hid behind the nearest tree and watched. I let out a sigh of relief as I saw Leah walk past. I stepped out and said, "Leah."

She spun around with wide eyes; her mouth fell open as she saw me.

I was certain I saw relief in her eyes, but she immediately became guarded and asked, "What are you doing here?"

I took a step toward her, but she stood back, I stopped, "I've come back for you."

Leah shook her head and looked away. She spoke softly, "I can't."

"Please Leah, I need you. I don't want to do this alone. The whole time we were apart, I just wished you were with me. I kept wanting to talk to you and have you by my side. Please come with me."

I could see the sadness in her eyes. She said, "I miss my mom so much. Rebecca reminds me of how I used to feel with my mom, it's something that I can't leave."

"I know you don't want to hear this, but it's not real. Rebecca isn't your mom and she can never take her place. Rebecca's just using you, she's hoping that Zilla will somehow switch with you. She doesn't care about you; look how she's been treating you. It's not right."

Leah's small shoulders began shaking as she cried. I knew I was hurting her, but I needed her to see the truth. I continued, "I just spoke with Dugal and he told me what Rebecca's been through. He said young women sense this hurt in Rebecca, and if they relate then it's very difficult to walk away. I know you miss your mom, but this isn't the way to deal with it."

The look in Leah's eyes broke my heart. I could see the young girl who had lost her mother way too early and had to grow up alone. With a father who didn't know how to deal with the tragedy and who got lost in the bottom of a bottle. She had to become the adult in the house and lost her own childhood, all the while ignoring the pain that ate at her heart.

Leah buried her face in her hands, "Who else do I have? I have no one. I'd rather have a false love than no love at all."

Unable to hold myself back any longer, I took three long strides and wrapped Leah in a hug. She didn't fight back, but instead cried into my shoulder. I stroked her hair and whispered, "You have me. I'm not going anywhere." She wrapped her hands around my waist, and we stood holding each other. Two broken people trying to be enough for each other. I just hoped that I would be enough for her.

Shouting split the air and broke the moment between us. We looked at each other in fear, Leah nodded, and I grabbed her hand as we started running. I dared a glance back and I saw Rebecca come crashing through the trees, her face was a twisted mask of fury and her eyes full of murder.

We were in the open and despite the stress of the situation, I couldn't help but smile that Leah was with me. We were back to facing the world together. It felt right. I let out a crazed laugh and shouted into the night air. The screams from Rebecca behind us only made me laugh louder. The quiet night air was interrupted by our shouts of freedom.

Shipwrecked

The rest of the journey had been uneventful, we didn't want to risk Rebecca catching up to us, so we continued walking through the night, but we never heard or saw anything of them again. I was still surprised to find that the light never disappeared completely and there was always enough to see where we were going.

I wondered if we were getting closer to the Prince's city, and if that was a good thing. We happily spotted the sea on the horizon and we quickened our pace. Despite not running for a while, we still held each other's hands, neither of us wanting to break the connection.

As we walked into the village, we both became aware of our hands clasped together and we smiled as we let go. My senses were filled with the smell of the salty air and there was also a hint of fish. Having grown up around trees and freshwater rivers, this was foreign to me. I could see the same look of awe on Leah's face. T

The houses were all faded white with porches that overlooked the bay. Despite having just walked in the village, we had a direct view to the water, as if all the houses were directing us where to go. I was shocked as I saw all the different shapes and sizes of boats in the water. I wondered how they all managed to get in and out of the bay without crashing into each other.

The nearer we got, the louder the shouting became. It wasn't shouts of anger, but it seemed like the normal way of communicating here. Out of the corner of my eye, I noticed a man wearing a blue suit, and sandals, watching us. The familiar sight calmed me slightly and I knew we were still going in the right direction. Leah noticed him too and we headed for him.

He greeted us warmly, if a bit loud, "Welcome to Mer, where we love the ocean and all the secrets that it contains. I'm glad to see you made it through the dreaded Audun." He shivered as if the name alone was too much for him, "Anyway, I'm sure you will find Mer a far greater adventure. Unfortunately, you can't stay in the village, but you can pick any of these ships to take you on your final journey to the Prince's city." He beamed with pride and the sound of water crashing intensified.

Leah and I looked at each other, I couldn't believe that we were a boat ride away from the city. I could feel my excitement rising.

The man quietened our excitement with his next words, "Just make sure that you choose the right captain. There are many options in the harbour, and each will take you to the city, but the leader of a ship has a big effect on how the journey will go." With that, he got up and disappeared among the people. I had questions, but I knew he wouldn't have answered them anyway.

"Oh great, what's the chance we're going to choose a good captain."

Leah nodded solemnly, "At least we know every ship is heading in the same direction, and now that we know what to look for, we just choose the Captain that feels right to both of us."

The next hour was a mixture of head scratching and indecision. All the crews of the ships were shouting at us and trying to sell their boat as the best one. I had worried that we would struggle to find someone to take us, but it was completely the opposite.

Everyone wanted us to board their ship and if we stood still for too long, they began ushering us aboard with extravagant promises. Some had the fastest ship around, others were the most luxurious, some had grand entertainment, they all promised the greatest journey was with them. We walked among many other people, who were all also trying to decide which ship to take.

Every now and again, you would see people walking on board and the entire crew would celebrate. And the next moment, the boat was pulling away.

Leah and I had decided to walk the length of the harbour, see all the ships, and then make our decision. We figured that this was the best strategy. But the farther we walked, the less sure I became. Each one sounded better than the last, and I wanted to try all of them. I wanted speed, but I also wanted something big and sturdy, and if the trip was going to be long, I would like something to keep us entertained.

I got so caught up in everything that they were offering that I kept forgetting to pay attention to the captain. Surely if the crew was happy, then they had an excellent captain. I groaned as we walked past a group of men promising us the finest food we had ever eaten, and as much as our hearts desired.

We reached the end of the harbour and saw a solid looking, not too large ship bobbing a little distance from the rest. No crew stood outside trying to convince us to board. Leah and I looked at each other in wonder. I knew we were thinking the same thing, but then I heard a call of the greatest collection of books. I said, "Maybe one more length of the harbour before we decide?"

Leah nodded absently as she heard the end of a promise of a vast art collection. We made our way back. All thoughts of the quiet ship lost in an overdose of promises. We walked the length of the harbour three more times and still we were no closer to making a decision. Neither of us were willing to commit to a single ship. The other issue was that as ships left, new ones would come in with new promises, so we felt that if we waited long enough, we would find the perfect one. But the perfect one never seemed to arrive.

My feet were hurting, and all the activity had given me a headache. This was the first headache I've had since leaving home. So much else had happened that I had forgotten about my headaches. I told Leah that I needed some quiet, "Maybe we could make our decision after we clear our heads."

We left the hubbub of the harbour and made our way to the far end. Again, we saw the same ship, with no one outside and no people bothering to get close. We spotted a bench with a beautiful view over the ocean, and I sat down with a sigh of relief.

I asked, "So what do you think? Which one should we take?"

Leah shrugged and massaged her temples, "There are too many options. How are we expected to choose?"

"Maybe we just choose one that we will both like? Like the food one, or we go for comfort, who knows how long we will have to be on the ocean for."

She groaned, "I can't choose! Each one promises us something better."

"I know. Let's just…"

Leah broke in, "What about this one?"

I looked at the quiet ship and wondered what they would offer us. Why was there no one outside? I hesitated, "It doesn't look like much is happening here. I don't want a ship that's going to be boring."

"Maybe that's exactly why we should take it? Take the option that seems least appealing."

I was doubtful, but I said, "Why not, maybe you're right." I got up and stretched, "Let's go look. Maybe they will have an endless supply of candy or something." After being promised so many wonderful things, I had high expectations.

We stood in front of the ship and called out. We waited for a response, but no sound came. I wondered if maybe it was deserted. I tried one last shout before we would head back to our bench. I was relieved. Up close, the ship looked worse for wear and I didn't want to travel on a rundown option.

But as soon as I shouted the final time, a crash came from within the ship. Loud calls for us to wait, and then a head appeared over us. All I saw was hair and eyebrows, before the man disappeared again. Leah had a small humoured grin; I could feel my own mouth hanging open.

A groan sounded and I was shocked to see that half the ship began falling towards us. We yelped in surprise and jumped backwards. It landed in front of us and the most interesting man I had ever seen came striding towards us. He had long grey hair that stood at impossible angles, long eyebrows, and a thick moustache that covered most of his mouth. His clothes were patched together with multiple colours but looked of fine quality. I liked him immediately. He reminded me of my uncle Telly.

The man bowed extravagantly, and I felt like clapping. His voice was deep, but clear, "I'm Forain, welcome to my ship, she is called Naufrage. We are delighted to have you call on us," He looked down the harbour and blew out his moustache, "Not many come our way." His eyebrows drew together, practically blinding him, and he seemed to forget we were here.

I cleared my throat, "So what are you offering?" Leah gave me a sharp look, but I ignored it. I was hoping for something good. I liked Forain, so I hoped he had something interesting for us.

Forain spread his arms, "I offer you my ship. Together we will travel to the city and it will be a great adventure."

My heart sank. I'd heard so many great promises, that I felt disappointed with just an offer of transport. I began to walk away, but Leah grabbed my arm and asked Forain, "What about your crew?"

"No crew, that will be you."

"Us? We won't know what to do?"

"That's untrue."

"We won't have a clue."

"It's good to learn something new."

Leah laughed, and Forain clapped his hands, "Young lady, you have the rhythm of a poet. Welcome aboard!" He flourished his coat and bowed to us.

Before I knew what was happening, Leah followed Forain onto the ship and she took his arm happily. I stood planted as I wondered what had just happened. The side of the ship creaked and began lifting. I yelped and jumped aboard as it slowly closed behind me.

I guess we had just found our captain for the journey.

Despite having to be the crew, I found that I really enjoyed being on a boat. I still wasn't sure if I was meant to call this a boat or a ship, I made a mental note to ask Forain later. Although he would probably want me to call it Naufrage. He walked around whispering to the ship as if it were a real person.

Forain was a great teacher. He never lost his temper and seemed to enjoy our fumbling. He would laugh heartily and then show us what to do. Once we made it to open water, we were each given turns manning the helm. He said it was a great honour to steer another man's ship.

It was an amazing feeling being in control of such a beautiful vessel, but the excitement soon wore off when

I was told to keep her straight, so I didn't have much to do. I looked over the ocean and marvelled at its size, I took a deep breath and enjoyed the fresh salty air after the staleness of the harbour.

I wondered where Clay was, and I felt a certainty that we were going to find him soon. I couldn't allow myself to think differently, although he could be anywhere, and the chance of us catching up with him seemed slim. I cleared my throat and focused on the motion of the swell swaying the ship.

Forain was walking with his hand caressing the rail of the ship. He seemed to be in a deep conversation with himself. Leah was standing on the other side, leaning on the rail and looking over the water. I wanted to go to her, but I had been given strict instructions never to leave the ship unmanned, so I sighed and watched Forain again. He had moved toward the centre beam that held the main sail and he was looking up. A frown pulled his thick eyebrows together.

I followed his gaze upward, but I couldn't see what he was looking at. A small flag flapped helplessly at the highest point, something was strange about the flag, but I couldn't put my finger on it. Forain was suddenly moving towards the front of the ship with an urgent stride.

I frowned and couldn't see anything different. The way ahead looked empty as it had the whole journey so far. I saw Forain sniffing the air and look back at the main sail. Leah had noticed the odd behaviour as well and was looking concernedly around us. I looked back at the sail and noticed that it seemed to be hanging uselessly, but as I watched, the sail pulled tight, but in the opposite direction. I suddenly realised that's what was wrong with the flag above, it was blowing in the opposite direction as us. The wind had changed direction.

Forain yelled and began tying and untying ropes all over the ship. He was a flurry of activity and Leah and I stood watching dumbstruck. Forain continued yelling, but I couldn't hear him over the sudden gust of wind that pushed me back a step. The steering wheel began spinning and I quickly jumped back to grab it.

I strained to hold as the wheel fought against me. I heard a loud crash and was shocked to see an enormous black cloud forming over the previously clear horizon. Suddenly the safety of the large ship seemed insignificant and I feared all the water around us.

I jumped in fright as I felt a hand on my shoulder. Forain had to speak into my ear for me to hear him, "I'll take over from here, boy. Go get the young lady and go below deck. I'll come call you when everything is safe again." I stepped back and watched Forain. His long hair was billowing behind him, and despite being mid-day, the sky had darkened.

Another loud clap of thunder sounded and a few seconds later, the sky lit up. In the light, I saw the urgency on Forain's face. He was trying to say something to me but I felt Leah grab me and I was pulled after her. We stumbled against each other as we made our way beneath deck. I felt sharp raindrops sting my face and arms. I struggled to pull the door shut and only with Leah's help managed to close it.

The thick wooden door blocked out the chaos outside and it fell eerily quiet. Leah's eyes were like saucers, "What are we going to do? Where did this come from, it was perfect a few minutes ago?"

I tried to remain calm for Leah's sake, but my voice wobbled anyway, "I don't know. I'm sure Forain knows what to do." I tried to shut out the fear I had seen in his eyes. The ship groaned as another loud clap of thunder came. Despite the warmth, Leah started shaking. I drew her into a hug, and we stood clinging to each other for comfort.

What felt like hours passed, and still the storm continued to rage. It was getting difficult to stand, so we moved to one of the secured couches. I was glad to see everything seemed to be nailed down and nothing inside was moving. We didn't speak, and the sound of the wind beating outside and the rain pelting the windows was the only thing that kept us company. My eyes slid shut as the ship continued to fight the storm.

A loud crash whipped my eyes open and I realised I must've dozed off. Light outside filled the windows, and I noticed the absence of the wind and rain. Leah yawned next to me, and she asked, "What happened? Is it over?"

"I think so." I let out a sigh of relief, "Where's Forain? I wonder how long the storm lasted."

We both made our way back onto the deck, but the destruction caused us both to stop. Pieces of the ship were thrown everywhere, and the sail was flapping uselessly on the floor. Even the ship seemed to lean to one side. We called for Forain, but there was no response. I noticed something else was different, but I couldn't think of what it was.

Leah revealed it to me, "We aren't moving anymore." She ran to the rail and her hand went to her mouth. I followed her and was shocked to find we were resting on land. The ship was still groaning, and another loud crack sent us both sprawling into the rail. Realising we needed to get off, I looked to my left and found a rope dangling off the side. Leah and I quickly made our way down and got a safe distance away.

"Where do you think Forain is?" Leah asked worriedly.

"I don't know, but I don't think he's on the ship anymore."

Leah chewed her fingernail, "I hope he's alright. Surely, he survived the storm, he got us to land safely." Tears filled her eyes, "This was meant to be a simple trip. I'm tired of things always going wrong."

I felt the same despair, but I forced myself to hide it. I looked around us. We were on a beach and wavy trees started a short distance from us. I wondered what this place was, and how we would get off. I took a look at the damage to the ship. I wouldn't be able to do anything about it, but I just needed to be doing something at the moment to distract myself from our new predicament.

The Last Leaf

The side we came down looked fine to me, and as I walked around, I was pleased to see the other side looked undamaged. Luckily, it was only the mast beam that was broken. I felt pleased with myself and more optimistic until I remembered how thick and tall that beam had been. There was no way I could even dream of fixing that. I looked back at Leah and wondered what we were going to do, I froze as I saw movement over her shoulder.

Fear filled me as I saw three people make their way toward her. I shouted and started running back to her. She looked over her shoulder, but instead of running away, she stood frozen in place. As I got nearer, I saw what kept Leah.

The men coming towards us wore flowing robes and all of them were completely bald. They looked like a group of monks. Their robes were brightly coloured, and I felt a stab of sorrow as it reminded me of Forain. What had happened to him? The men all had open, kind faces and looked to be in their late fifties.

As they neared us, they tilted their heads in greeting. A man who radiated authority spoke, "Welcome weary travellers. I am Chef, and these are my two wonderful friends, Aatif and Priyan."

Aatif said, "Welcome Lino."

Priyan spoke, "Welcome Leah."

They again bowed their heads in greeting. Leah and I were so shocked by their appearance and presence that we both didn't respond. Chef smiled to himself and looked over our shoulder. He said, "I'm surprised you got onto a ship called Naufrage. The name alone speaks of its destiny."

I found my voice, "How do you know it's called Naufrage? And how did you know our names."

Chef smiled warmly. He reminded me of Santa. Except that other than his eyebrows, he had no hair on his head. I nearly laughed at the oddity of the thought. Chef said, "We have met the ship and captain before. Actually, the situation was rather similar to this one as well."

"So, this has happened before?" I spluttered.

Priyan answered, "The name destined the journey."

Leah asked, "So what does the name mean?"

The three men laughed and Aatif said, "Naufrage means shipwreck."

Chef continued, "But do not worry, we will have it fixed up in no time for you. In the meantime, it would be an honour to have you stay with us. We do not have many visitors, so this is a very special day indeed."

I still couldn't believe that we had chosen a ship that was named shipwreck. It had seemed like the right option. The safe option. I wondered what the other ships would've held.

Leah seemed to also have found her voice again. She asked, "What about Forain? Do you know what happened to him? We can't find him anywhere."

Chef smiled again, "He will show up when the ship is ready. Nothing keeps him away from his ship for long, but he conveniently misses all the hard work." He laughed and motioned for us to follow him. Since we didn't have any other option, we followed without any complaint.

Devon Hoole

The Elders

It was a short journey through wavy trees and small rounded bushes dotted between them. We walked into a village that looked like something I would've imagined as a young child. We first saw a cleared area with a large firepit in the centre and wooden logs as seating. The longer I looked, the more you began to see.

Hanging between many of the trees were hammocks, but I also noticed that many of them were bridges that connected structures up in the trees. I was delighted to see that the village was one giant network of tree houses. But instead of feeling disconnected from the ground, everything seemed to happily meld into one another.

It was difficult to tell where the houses ended, and the ground began. The next thing I noticed was that all the people were dressed in a similar fashion to Chef, and even seemed to be the same age as him. I didn't see any children running around or any sign of youth.

Yet despite the older age group, everyone walked with a light step and there was an air of energy among the people. Chef turned to us and smiled broadly, he said, "Welcome to our humble home. We do not have many visitors, but we are always glad at their arrival."

He led us through the small village and introduced us to anyone who happened to be walking past. Each person greeted us with a hug and a warm smile. It felt like we were in the happiest old age home I had ever experienced. Their hugs and brief anecdotes made me feel like I was back home chatting with my grandparents. Leah was already smiling and laughing with a group of older ladies. It was a surreal experience, and I was loving every second of it.

Chef whispered to me, "Let's give the ladies some space, I have something I want to show you."

A last glance at Leah surrounded by happy chatter told me she would be fine. She caught my eye and we grinned at each other. Then I turned and followed the large man. I felt like a small child happily following his father, Chef towered over me and I had to put a skip in my step to keep up with him. I asked, "So what is this place? Where are all the young people?"

Chef roared with laughter, a full belly sound that made me grin stupidly, he said, "Where are the young people you say? What makes you think we are old?" He raised an eyebrow at me.

I spluttered awkwardly and tried to think of a response, but Chef clapped me on the shoulder and chuckled, "I understand what you mean." He looked around and lowered his voice, "I wouldn't say that too loudly around the others, they aren't as young as the two of us and might get offended." Chef looked in his mid-sixties and I frowned.

He roared again and gave me a light push, "You have an honest face, that's good. Although my ego would've preferred a better liar."

"Sorry." I grinned. I noticed that the temperature had dropped slightly as we were walking. Large leafy trees were around us and their broad leaves hung in our path. I looked down and realised that we were walking on a thick moss. A slight mist hung in the air and I could feel the dampness on my skin. I felt the tension leaving my body and I took a deep breath; the air was sweet and filled my lungs with a crisp coolness.

Chef stopped, grabbed a towel and pair of shorts from the cleft of a tree. He handed the pair to me and took another for himself. Confused, I asked, "What's this for?"

He put his fingers to his lips and motioned for me to change. I hesitated, but then decided that I would trust Chef. I shivered as I changed, the temperature had dropped further, and my hair was already damp from the mist. Once we were both in our swimming shorts, Chef led me further into the draping trees. The moss on the floor tickled my feet, but it felt soft to the touch. The mist continued to thicken until I could only see the outline of the big man in front of me. I stopped as I saw Chef begin shrinking and seemingly sink into the earth. I looked down and realised that my feet were in water and warmth ran up my legs.

I took a few more steps forward and the water deepened. The warm water gently lapped against my skin, but other than that there was no disturbance on the surface. I saw Chef's bauld head bobbing in the water, and he motioned for me to follow. I took hesitant steps but moving deeper filled me with further warmth and I shivered in pleasure. The ground beneath my feet was soft, but my steps were secure, and I didn't fear slipping. My feet left the floor and I swam the last few spans to Chef.

Chef whispered, "This is a very special place, we use this as a place to meditate and receive clarity. Sometimes it's important to be quiet and listen, give our minds some time to re-organise and process what we've been ignoring." He smiled and then lay his head back and floated contently with eyes closed.

I looked around and found that I could see more clearly just above the water, and there seemed to be rocks all around us. We were in a large rock pool and warm steam was rising from the water. I took a deep breath and felt my mind clearing, all thoughts concentrated, and my focus became single-minded. It was as if the water was wanting me to do something and was gently nudging my thoughts in the correct direction.

I remembered what Chef said to me about giving my mind some time to process things. That thought flittered away and I was left with silence and nothingness. I tilted my head back and felt my body rise to the surface. I was suddenly floating contently on the water.

It was as if a wall had suddenly been built around my mind and no thoughts were allowed in. For the first time in my life, I was not overthinking situations or criticising myself, it was a blissful silence. Warm water covered my ears, and I became aware of my heart beating. The consistent thud of every beat reminded me of the source of my existence.

I took another deep breath and felt myself relax further. The tensions of the past few weeks began loosening and leaving my body. The steady pounding of my heart slowed down further. In the fortress of my mind, I began hearing noises between each beat, I strained to hear what they were. The flutter of curiosity breaking into my consciousness increased my heart rate. The thumping drowned out the noise.

Nothing but the drum of life, I breathed deeply and relaxed. Again, everything slowed, and the noise increased between each beat. Each time I focused on the foreign sounds, my heartbeat would quicken and drown it out. I decided to ignore the noise and see what happens. The sounds increased, but instead of focusing on them, I emptied my mind and allowed it to become white noise.

I thought I recognised voices, but I focused on my breathing and clearing my mind. Suddenly, in my mind's eye, I was drawn up into the air and I could see over the walls that were in my mind. All the noise was revealed, and I saw memories playing out beyond the wall. It was chaotic, some were clear and easy to identify, while others were blurry and filled with painful emotion. Some overlapped with each other, while others were far off in the distance. I noticed a large black cloud was hanging over a certain group of memories.

A doorway appeared in the wall, and suddenly all the memories rushed towards it trying to get through. On the edge of my thoughts, I wondered what would happen if they all got through, but this slipped away, and I was back to watching disconnected from a distance. A memory slipped through and began playing out in front of me.

Clay looked about nine years old and I was seven. We were in the small forest behind our house and were playing in a stream that had appeared after a heavy rainfall. Both of us had a small leaf boat that we had created, and we got ready for the race. Clay counted down and the race began.

From my omniscient position I watched as my younger self jumped up and down as my boat pulled ahead. I didn't often win at anything and so this was exciting for me. As the finish line neared, Clay's heavy boot came crashing down on my boat. His boat slowly floated past the finish line and he smugly smiled and cheered at his victory.

The first awareness of emotion reached me, and I ground my teeth. My younger self burst into tears and took off back towards the house. Clay shouted and ran after me. Our size difference made Clay catch up quickly and I watched as we both tumbled to the ground. Clay pinned me and asked, "Where are you going? You're not crying because you lost, are you?"

"Leave me alone!" My little legs flailed as I tried to break free, and the tears continued streaming down my face.

Clay shook me and shouted, "Stop being such a baby!"

"I'm telling mom, you always do this. You never let me win, I hate you!"

I could see the hurt flash across Clay's eyes, but he tried to hide it by appearing uninterested. He got off me and started walking away, "Fine, run to mom then. Just know that I'll never play with you again."

I lay on the ground snivelling, torn between my desire to tell on Clay, but also fearing his threat. I looked over and saw my crushed boat bumping into a log, and my anger flared again. I got up and marched off towards the house. The scene jumped to my mom shouting at Clay and sending him off to his room.

The look he gave me before he left said a thousand words. The memory darkened, and I was sleeping in my bed. A dark figure appeared over me and quietened my scream with a hand over my mouth.

Clay leant in and whispered, "I hate you. You hear me, I'll never forgive you for telling mom. You better never talk to me again, or I'll do more than squash your stupid boat." The memory dissipated.

Before I could process what had happened, a new memory was shoving its way through the door. The dark cloud was coming nearer, but the memory pulled my attention. It was a few years later and Clay and I were both standing in front of our father. He was furious and was pointing at a smashed window. My dad was adamant about owning up to your mistakes and he expected the culprit to come forward.

Despite honesty, no mercy would be shown, so we were often too scared to tell the truth. I looked over at Clay and he gave me a desperate look. We both knew who had really broken the window, but Clay had been getting into trouble more often lately and he couldn't be caught making another mistake. My loyalty to my brother won out, and I took the blame.

Again, night came in the memory and I was sniffling into my pillow. A dark figure appeared in my room, but instead of bringing fear, it brought comfort. Clay rubbed my back, "Are you alright? Thanks for saying you broke the window. You know how dad would've killed me. I really appreciate it."

I tried to smile and spoke through shuddering breaths, "It wasn't so bad."

"Thanks Lino." Clay gave me a hug. The memory lightened in happiness and then dissipated.

I remembered that was the first time I felt like I had won Clay's love back. I loved pleasing him and seeing how happy he was whenever I did something he liked, but whenever I questioned him or disagreed with what he was doing, I would see the flash of anger in his eyes and immediately I would change my mind. I couldn't bear to have him angry at me again.

I started taking more blame for things he would do, and each time he would give me a slap on the shoulder and make me feel like a hero. My life became focused on earning Clay's approval, and I tried to become someone he accepted.

The cloud was nearly over the walls. A loud bang sounded, and I saw cracks spiderweb in every direction. The walls of my mind split open and memories started piling in. Too many played out at the same time that I couldn't concentrate on a single one.

My emotions were pulled in every direction as different scenarios in my life filled my mind. It was such a jumble of feelings that I didn't know what I was feeling or what to make of it. Except one thing became clearer, I noticed that Clay seemed to make an appearance in all of them. I looked up and saw the cloud was now completely covering my walls, raindrops began to fall and as they landed on the memories, each memory seemed to flicker, and everything became more confused.

My mom's voice rang out over the chaos, "Where did my boy go?"

Other voices called out for Clay, I heard my own among them. Rain continued to fall and soon the ground was filling with water. The water continued to rise, and everything became numbed out. It became difficult to get my thoughts moving again, and I felt like my mind was being crushed by the weight of the water. I was convinced that I was about to die.

Just as quickly as it started, the water began to empty. The pressure lessened and I looked around to see what had happened. The walls around my mind were left in ruins and a man was standing where the door used to be. Light surrounded him, but I couldn't make out his face. I tried to call out to him, but a hand on my shoulder pulled me out of my meditative state.

I opened my eyes and stared into the sky in confusion. Blue sky filled my vision, and it took me a few moments to reorient myself. I remembered that I was lying in a warm pool on some island after we got shipwrecked. All the mist was gone, as if used up. Everything snapped back into focus and I frowned at the odd experience I'd just had. Despite being able to see more clearly, my mind now felt fogged with mist.

Chef was talking to me, "Lino, it's time to head back. We need to prepare for the feast."

I numbly nodded and we swam back to the shore. The walk back was silent as I contemplated everything that had just happened. I wasn't ready to talk yet, but I knew I needed to ask Chef about what had just happened. I knew something significant had taken place, but it wasn't over yet, and I needed to go back to see who that man was. I already felt the pull towards the calming waters.

I watched Lino walk away with Chef and then disappear among the trees. I smiled to myself as I thought of Lino and everything he was beginning to mean to me. From a distance, I'd had a crush on him for a while, but this journey, despite its heartaches and challenges, has shown me his deeper side. He's slowly lowered his defences and allowed me to see what's behind the walls he keeps up. Having him come back and convince me to leave Rebecca had meant so much. It was difficult for me to trust people and feel as though I could rely on someone, but his coming back had shown me that he could be someone I could trust.

I grimaced at the thought of Rebecca and how easily I had been drawn into her spell. I could still feel the desire to go back and try make it work. The need to be loved by a motherly figure was strong, and I now realised that I couldn't pretend that I was fine any longer.

Tears filled my eyes and I quickly looked away before the other ladies could see. A woman who looked to be in her sixties, reached out and gave my arm a squeeze. I remembered her name as Amor. As with every lady here, she wore a scarf that held her hair back. She had thick curly black hair that seemed to be fighting the scarf for freedom, sharp features, and eyes that spoke of kindness.

Amor whispered, "Let's go, I need your help with something." She called the other ladies and we all walked a short distance through the odd village.

I still wondered why all the houses were off the ground and in the trees. It was beautiful though, seeing nature and humans seemingly blend so effortlessly. We reached the outskirts, although it was hard to tell, and another smaller open area appeared before us. Soft grass covered the ground, but it looked worn down, as if an army of people had walked through.

I looked at Amor questioningly, she smiled mischievously as she walked to the centre. She looked me dead in the eye, stamped her feet twice and then struck a pose. My mouth hung open in surprise and they all started laughing at my expression. The others made their way to Amor, and as they entered the circle, their movements became more fluid. I stared in wonder at the beauty and strength that each woman held herself with.

They formed a circle and started clapping their hands and stomping their feet in a steady rhythm. My heart sank as I was reminded of the nights I had spent dancing with Rebecca and her family. But somehow this felt different and all thoughts of dread were quickly dispelled. I felt the ground vibrate beneath my feet and each beat awakened something inside me, something I had ignored for a long time, but had always secretly desired.

Amor broke free from the circle and walked towards me, she took my hand and I walked on leaden legs as she led me to the others. To my horror, she led me into the centre of the circle. She took my hands and kissed each one, she also kissed me on the forehead. The look in her eyes filled me with courage and the pounding of the earth seemed to match my heartbeat.

Amor moved back to her position in the circle. I was surrounded by at least twenty women, all who were moving and stomping in unison. The circle tightened around me, and each woman linked arms, becoming a unified body of dancers.

The strength of the sound and the bond between the women filled me with emotion. Tears were already streaming down my face. I felt like crawling into a ball and hiding away, but instead I kept my head held high and faced the circle. I saw a few nods of approval. The circle of woman began moving clockwise around me.

The steady beat increased in pace and I sensed the urgency in what they were doing. My heartrate increased and I was reminded of the fearful moments when I had felt vulnerable and in need of protection. The main thought was sitting at my mother's funeral and feeling completely alone. My tears fell heavily.

The circle of women continued spinning around me, but now they began pulsating in and out. Each movement inwards felt like a blow to my heart. I was reminded of all the times I wished my father would stop drinking and be there for me. The rush of memories nearly threatened to bring me to my knees, but I fought to stay on my feet.

Suddenly colour was all around me as all the ladies loosened the scarves from their hair. Amor broke free from the circle and made her way towards me. She used her scarf to dry a tear on my cheek and then she wrapped the scarf around my body, tying it off. Before leaving, she gave me a strong hug.

More ladies approached and wiped a tear before tying the scarf and giving me a hug. My body shook with grief as I felt the cocoon begin to form around me. Soon my vision was blinded as a scarf was tied around my eyes. After the last hug, I felt the tightness of the scarves and found that it was difficult to breathe.

All of a sudden, the stomping stopped, and silence filled the air. The pressure continued to increase around me, and I was convinced that if I didn't break free from this, I would be crushed. I began struggling against my bonds and the stomping started up again. Slowly at first, but the more I struggled, the faster the rhythm became. Shouts of encouragement rose from the circle as I continued to fight.

My life had been a struggle and I had felt trapped for so long, and I knew I needed to break free from this to prove to myself that I was strong enough. My arms began tiring and my breath was coming in gasps, but I fed off the energy from the women around me and slowly I felt the scarves begin to loosen.

My first arm broke free and a roar of approval came from the circle. My other arm came out and the shouts of encouragement became deafening. As each scarf fell to the floor, I felt a weight being lifted off me and an inner pressure was loosened. I left the scarf around my eyes for last. I took a deep breath and took it off.

Light filled my vision, temporarily blinding me. In the light, I saw a man standing in front of me and he was cheering. As my eyes adjusted, he disappeared while walking away with a woman that looked like an older version of me. My heart leapt and I nearly cried out for them to stop, but the picture was gone and all I saw was all the women rushing towards me.

I looked down at my hands in wonder. I felt new, like something that had held me for a long time had finally broken off and now I was free to be myself again. A stronger, new version of the person I had been a few moments ago. I was enveloped in hugs and pats on the back. Each woman had tears on her cheeks and pride filled their eyes.

After lots of laughing and happy chatter, Amor spoke, "Leah, you have displayed immense strength, and we are all extremely proud of you. Remember what happened here today and know that you don't need to be afraid any longer. Our stories are what make us strong, you don't need to hide from your past anymore."

My mom's face floated across my eyes and I still felt a sadness, but it was no longer debilitating, it was the natural sense of loss from losing a loved one. I smiled as I said goodbye to my mom and thanked her for the time we'd had together. The part of me that stopped living and that had held me back from moving on, was suddenly no longer there. It felt as if I had truly shed my old self and I was new, the constraints I had placed on my life, had broken off and now I could experience growth again.

I said as much to Amor, and she smiled, "It's amazing what can happen when we are surrounded by people who support us and believe in us. I remember when I was in the centre of the circle. I think I cried for days afterwards. For some, it brings resolution, but for others, it shows us what we have been ignoring and that can often be just as painful. Let us sit and talk for a while. It's good to hear the testimonies of others."

I happily sat down and soon all the other ladies were comfortably sprawled across the ground. My heart lifted even higher as we laughed and shared with one another. It was the first time I truly felt content and at peace in a long time.

🌿 🌿 🌿

I spent the rest of the afternoon in a numbed state. My eyes were open, but I wasn't taking in much of what was going on. I spoke to people, but my words seemed to come from someone else. I felt disconnected from everything around me. I looked up and saw Leah coming. My heart fluttered at the sight of her, and for the first time since the mysterious pool, I felt joy breaking through again.

She smiled as she saw me, and I grinned goofily back. Impossibly, her hair seemed to have grown in the time we'd been here, and it swung freely behind her back. Her dark eyes that had previously looked haunted, now shone with an energy and she even seemed to walk with a lighter step. She sat down next to me and I was pleased with how close she was.

"How are you?"

I was lost in her eyes; something had definitely changed. Her presence was shutting my brain down further and I was sure my mouth was hanging open.

I saw the hint of a smile touch her lips, but she continued, "I just had the most amazing time." She looked around and breathed deeply, "There is something about this place. I don't know what it is, but the people here…" She fell silent as if lost in thought. She looked at me again and smiled, "How's your day been?"

"What's happened to you? Something has changed?"

Leah laughed softly, and playfully looked at me out of the corner of her eye, as if deciding if I was ready to hear an exciting secret. She said, "It's difficult to explain, but I was wrapped in scarves and I had to fight my way out.

I was in the centre of a circle of ladies and they all helped me heal from the loss of my mother."

"Scarves?"

Leah laughed again, "I don't know how it happened, it was more symbolic than anything else, but it feels as if I've shed the old me and now, I'm someone new. I needed the space to properly process my mom's death and I hadn't allowed myself to do that, but this seemed to be that final push I needed. I realised that I'm stronger because of what I've been through and although I still miss my mom terribly, I will be okay without her."

Leah's eyes shone brighter, and she took my hand, "I wish I had done this earlier, if only someone had talked me through this, I could've been spared a lot of heartache. It would've made the decision to keep living easier." She shook her head and said, "I've been talking too much, now tell me what happened with you? You look a bit shell-shocked."

I looked at our hands intertwined together, and I smiled at how far we'd come. From trying to scare her in the forest at home for following me, and then our constant fighting the whole journey, but now she was the only other person I felt I could rely on. It was a special connection we now had. She gave my hand a squeeze and I finally voiced my experience.

As I spoke it felt as if it had all happened to someone else. But the more I spoke, the less numb I felt. I appreciated how Leah gave me her full attention and didn't interrupt with questions. I didn't think I would be able to finish if I was stopped. I finally told her about the water rising, how I felt being crushed, and then the man that I saw.

Leah's eyes widened at the mention of the man, but still she kept her silence. I finished my story and fell silent, feeling emotionally drained. I watched Leah as she processed what I'd said, her lips moved, and I could see her mind racing. A flash of sympathy crossed her eyes but was gone in an instant. She seemed hesitant to ask, but she said, "So most of your memories were about Clay?"

I nodded and Leah grimaced as if I'd confirmed something for her, but before I could read too much into what she was asking, she said, "I also saw a man. When the final scarf fell from my eyes, and I was briefly blinded by the light, I saw a man cheering. The light seemed to come from him, it was amazing."

That sounded familiar to my experience, "Who do you think he is?"

Leah frowned in concentration and then said, "I'm not sure, but I think it might've been the Prince." At the mention of the Prince, the trees seemed to creak in praise, and a gentle wind whistled through the leaves.

I looked around in wonder, the world around us continued to respond to any mention of the Prince. Again, I was left wondering who this person was and what sort of power he had, if even nature responded to his name. I still wasn't sure if I trusted him, "What does he want with us?"

Leah shook her head, but I got this sense that she was not telling me everything. She avoided my eyes, but her thumb was massaging my hand as if trying to comfort me. She said softly, "Your experience sounds similar to mine."

I shook my head about to interrupt, but Leah continued, "Think about it. You heard the thumping of your heart; I had the ladies stomping their feet. You felt this wall around your mind; I had a circle of women around me. You had memories of your brother; I thought about my mom. We both felt like we were being crushed, but then it disappeared, and we saw the man."

I conceded, "Okay, that sounds similar if you put it like that, but then why do you feel so great and I feel like I've been run over by a truck."

Leah pursed her lips in thought. She seemed to think out loud, "Maybe I was ready to let go and say goodbye, but you aren't ready yet."

I felt like I was missing the importance of what she was saying, my thoughts were hitting up against something and I couldn't properly process her words, "Why would I need to say goodbye? I don't understand."

Tears filled her eyes, and she turned so that she was facing me fully, "Lino, I'm not sure if we're going to find Clay. He might be…"

Finally it clicked what she was trying to say, "No no no, that's not right. I don't believe that for a second. Clay is here and I'm going to find him. That's the whole point of this journey! We've been doing all this so I can bring him back home. There's no way that this has all been for nothing. I won't believe it!"

Leah still looked doubtful and seemed to believe I was denying the obvious. My mind raced and then I excitedly said, "But I've seen him! Yes, I saw him for the first few days that we were here. Don't you remember? I kept telling you I was sure he was around. He's here, I know it." I said the last part with extra feeling. I was going to find my brother and bring him home.

"But then why were all your memories about him? Surely it means something important, the lake was trying to help you process difficult information." She paused and swallowed, "I saw my mom walk away with the Prince at the end…," The trees rustled again in response to the Prince's name, Leah continued unaware, "…as if he was taking the pain of her memory away. Maybe you have gotten stuck somewhere and need his help to say goodbye." She fell silent and looked worried that she had gone too far.

I shook my head, "I refuse to believe it. Then why have we had this opportunity to catch him? I have always had a strange feeling about this Prince," Nature responded again by making noise, but this time I had a different thought. Maybe it wasn't praise that made them move, maybe it was something else. I said, "If we can get to

Clay before he reaches the Prince, then I'm sure that it'll all be fine."

I stood up and offered my hands to Leah, "I heard they're making a feast for us, so let's try enjoy that, and then hopefully we can leave tomorrow." She sighed but took my hands and we walked towards the fire that was already blazing. People were happily chatting amongst themselves.

The feast was soon underway and all worried thoughts about Clay were quickly abated. Despite the light barely dimming, the atmosphere was festive, and everyone was full of energy. I still marvelled that the light didn't seem to be going away anymore. It made me lose track of time a long time ago. We ate so many types of fish that I couldn't keep up and different breads that all smelled heavenly.

The food was passed around and we ate with our fingers. Each time a new basket of food passed by; I couldn't resist but try. I must've eaten my weight in bread and fish, when eventually I couldn't have anything more. Leah was happily talking to anyone around us and I smiled at how she radiated with her new confidence.

Despite trying to engage with those around me, I found that my mind was wandering back to the lake. I needed to see what it all meant and try to uncover what secrets it held. I got up and stretched, saying that I needed to walk off some of the food. Once out of view, I quickly collected my towel and headed back in the direction of the water.

Soon the mist was back, and I felt the shiver of anticipation, although I couldn't ignore the seed of fear that sat in my stomach as well. I found the tree and changed, then slowly headed into the water. The warm water gently lapped against me and I breathed the calming air in deeply. I tilted my head back and felt my legs rise to the surface, I allowed my thoughts to wander.

Minutes passed and nothing happened. I forced myself to focus on my breathing and to allow my muscles to relax. Still nothing changed. After another ten minutes, I angrily raised my head and looked around, "Why isn't this working?" I was met with the calm silence of the unsettled water.

I slapped the water with my arms and shouted, "I need to know what all this means! Why is this happening? Tell me!" I fell silent but there was no other sound other than a trickle of falling water nearby. Shaking my head, I headed back to the shore. I felt worse than before, now wondering if I would ever get answers.

Ever since Clay caught the leaf and came here, nothing has made sense anymore. I needed to find him and go back home; I needed some normality back in my life. A deep tiredness settled in my bones and I wondered how much longer I could do this. As I neared the feast, I heard music and laughter. Dimmed shapes moved elegantly in time with the music. I sighed at the sight of more dancing. Part of me wanted to join in and forget all my thoughts, but I knew I could never do that. Instead, I kept hidden.

Despite not feeling tired, I found myself drifting off and the world around me fell away. Unsure if minutes had passed or hours, I heard Leah whispering my name. I opened my eyes and smiled as I saw her. Her eyes glittered with excitement and shone even more than before.

She gripped my arm and said, "The elders are calling us."

I rubbed my eyes, "Who are the elders?" I noticed that the light was the same dim.

"They are, everyone here." Leah was pulling me to my feet in her excitement, "They are going to speak over us."

"What does that mean?"

"I'm not exactly sure." She laughed and her eyes sparkled. She yanked my hand, "Let's go! Quickly!" Leah practically ran back towards the village with me in tow.

We approached the area where the bonfire had burned, but now instead of music and dancing, everyone was seated facing the same way. I cringed as I saw two wooden seats facing everyone. I wondered if we were about to go on trial, it definitely looked like it. Leah led me straight to the front and happily took a seat, she motioned for me to do the same. I looked out over all the aged faces, some wore happy smiles while others had far off looks in their eyes,

Chef and Amor stood up and addressed us. Amor spoke first, "Usually we would speak over people individually, but since you started this journey together, we felt it more fitting that you receive this together."

Chef continued, "We would like to give you some encouragement before you leave us and continue your journey." His eyes flickered toward me, "Sometimes our struggles feel more than we can bear, but there is always a way out and hope is often just around the corner."

A drop of hope flickered in my heart as I wondered at his words. Chef and Amor spoke in unison, "Let's begin." Their words cut through the air and rang out with authority. Suddenly, everything seemed more important and the weight of what was coming settled around us.

An aged man stood up, who looked as weather worn as a tree trunk, but his eyes were kindly, and his voice rang out clearly, "I must be loved by everyone in my life, and by everyone that I meet." He remained standing.

A lady with snow white hair stood, "My past determines my present behaviour and I'm trapped living a life I wish I could change." She also remained standing.

Another lady with close cropped red hair rose and spoke, "I have to be perfect in everything I do, that is the only way I will believe that I am worthy of being loved."

People continued to speak and then remain standing. Each one said something that reverberated in my head and lined up perfectly with words I had often told myself. These were my darkest thoughts spoken aloud. Some spoke of a deep loneliness, and the fear of being alone, others wondered if they would ever amount to anything, or if their life would have a purpose.

Each line hit me in the chest and made my head ring. I wasn't sure how much more of this I could take as they continued sharing one by one. Their words swam around in my head and I felt as if each person was laying a heavy chain over my shoulders. The speaking continued.

"What's my next step?"

"Am I worthy of being loved?"

"What happens after all this?"

I heard Leah crying next to me, and I realised that tears were falling down my cheeks as well. I wished for them to stop. These thoughts were destructive.

"I deserve everything I've gotten."

"Is my life even worth living?"

"Will anyone even care if I'm gone?"

Through my blurred vision, I saw that half the elders were standing. Chef's voice rang out again, "I come before you and expose these for what they are. Every word spoken has been a lie created to destroy you. Our thoughts have more power than we can imagine. Let the truth ring out with a loud voice and dispel these lies."

I sat rocking back and forth with my head in my hands. The weight of despair was pulling me down and I needed it to end. I looked up as Chef finished speaking, something seemed to have shifted in the atmosphere. The air suddenly crackled as if a battle was about to take place. Those who had spoken first, turned and faced the rest of the elders.

A barrel-chested man stood and faced the first man who had spoken, "I was created to be loved, and the one who knows me will never stop loving me." A loud crack sounded, and the weather worn man sat down.

Another stood and addressed the white-haired lady, "I'm not a victim of my past, I am stronger for it and will decide my own future." Another loud bang and she took a seat.

"I will try my best in everything I do, but my worth does not come from perfection. I am who I am and I'm not ashamed of that." The red-haired lady slumped into her seat.

Each new person stood and addressed the lie that was told. Every time, the new thought remained, and the old was forced away. I felt the blow of each new truth, and they rang powerfully in my mind. The weight around my neck seemed to fall off with each victory.

"I will bring light wherever I go."

"I am a victor."

Their words filled me with hope and strength. It felt like I was finally eating after being starved my entire life, and all my energy flowed back into me. The tiredness was replaced, and I squeezed my hands together as if holding onto every word spoken.

"I am designed for a purpose."

"I am chosen and destined for life."

I began repeating every sentence, and each time it seemed to tighten around me, as if armouring me for the journey ahead. The last voice fell silent, but then Amor and Chef came and stood before us.

Amor spoke, "Your thoughts are powerful forces that can either help you soar to new heights or they will pull you down into the deepest pits. Remember what you heard here today; you both have something special inside of you. Don't allow anyone to tell you differently."

Everyone fell silent and I took deep breaths trying to make sense of what had just happened. We spent a few minutes in silence as we processed the elder's words.

Chef motioned for us to stand, "Unfortunately, our time together has ended. Your ship has been repaired and Forain is waiting for you. He is eager to be off. Thank you for spending this time with us. Although it has been short, we all have enjoyed it thoroughly." All the elders stood and began clapping and cheering.

I looked around in bewilderment, this whole experience was too weird to understand. Leah rushed into Amor's arms and hugged her fiercely. I shook Chef's hand, but I couldn't resist asking, "Please tell me about Clay. Will I find him? I know you know who he is and what's happening, please tell me."

Chef sadly shook his head, "It's not my place to tell. You'll find all your answers once you reach the Prince's city." He spoke with a finality that told me he would say no more.

I sighed but inclined my head in thanks, "Thank you. I'll never forget what happened here today." I could still feel their words bouncing around in my head. The despair I had felt earlier was a distant memory, and I was filled with hope for the journey forward.

Chef gave my hand one last squeeze, "Lino, it's time for the two of you to finish this journey."

The Prince's City

Forain met us energetically, if a bit sheepishly, and wrapped us up in hugs and tales of heroism on his part to get back to us, and I couldn't help but smile at his presence. I asked, "Forain, do you know that Naufrage means shipwreck?"

He nibbled on part of his moustache and muttered about us needing to leave the island quickly. Leah and I looked at each other and laughed. We boarded the ship and waved our goodbyes. The island and the elders were quickly lost to our sight, and I realised that this would be the first place that I would miss.

No one had tried to trick us or hurt us, it was the first safe haven we'd had this entire journey and I wondered if there was a reason for it, was something worse coming up ahead.

I was back behind the wheel, with strict instructions to keep her straight. I swallowed and nervously looked around, hoping that a sudden storm wouldn't appear. I glanced at Leah and Forain talking animatedly and wondered what would happen to us after this journey was over.

Would everything go back to normal or would we continue with what had started between us? I felt like I'd grown so much, but would it be enough. Would this be enough to help me leave my house more often, or would I sink back into my solitary lifestyle? The elder's words rattled in my mind and I realised that my thoughts were heading down an unfruitful path.

"I'll be different. I'm going to fight for what I want."

"And what's that?"

I jumped in fright and turned red as Leah came up next to me. She wore a smirk that said she knew what I was thinking, and her eyes sparkled. I spluttered, trying to think of something clever to say. Luckily, I was saved by Forain's shout.

He stood looking over the water and swept his arms for us to see, "Welcome to the City of the Prince."

The water suddenly sounded louder, and the wind gave a gust of air. I shivered at the thought of being this close to the Prince. The answers I sought were up ahead and

I wondered if I would like the answers. I also clung to the hope that Clay would be there, and we would finally be able to go home.

I put my arm around Leah and said, "Clay is up ahead. We'll soon be back together and be able to go home." Leah wore a worried frown, but she kept her silence. A sliver of doubt crept back in, but I quickly squashed it and quietened the voice.

My eyes widened as the city came fully into view. Large golden bridges connected several islands together. Each island seemed covered in palaces and large estates, it was impossibly spacious and yet overcrowded at the same time. The buildings were all beautifully built and were covered in intricately carved shapes and symbols.

Each one was designed differently, as if everyone was asked what their dream home would look like, and then given the freedom to build it. Despite the differences, there was no mistaking that they were all built by the same hand. There was a familiarity and fitting of every building that spoke of a skilled master. The longer I looked, it seemed that every building was connected in some way, as if they were truly one house.

My eyes were pulled to the centre island, and it seemed that every other building was only there to heighten the beauty of this one. Large marble pillars formed a circle around a domed building that glinted golden in the light. I frowned as the light seemed to emit from the building. Everything looked open and easily accessible, as if anyone was welcome at any time. The light seemed to draw me in, and I immediately knew that was where the Prince would be.

Shouts from Forain pulled me out of my reverie, and I jumped to begin helping dock the ship. I sighed in relief as I saw men waiting to help us. Quickly we were landed, and the ropes were securely tied. Forain came up to us and gave us another big hug. His big mound of hair tickled my noise and caused me to sneeze. We both laughed and hugged again.

Forain scratched his head and said, "Well, I guess this is goodbye. It's been a pleasure. Lino, I hope you find your brother. Leah, continue to let your inner poet out." His voice caught and he loudly cleared his throat, "Anyway, sorry about our little detour. I doubt I'm ever going to have anyone on my ship again." He looked at us with such defeat that I couldn't help but save him.

I said, "As far as I'm concerned, it was the greatest adventure I could've asked for. And I learnt something along the way. Everything was delivered as promised." Leah voiced her agreement.

Forain stopped nibbling his moustache and grinned widely. I knew it was wide, because it was the first time I saw a flash of teeth. Standing on the deck, all his flamboyance was back, and he bowed to us extravagantly. A loud groaning sounded, and half the ship fell out towards the docks.

We walked onto the land with our last waves to Forain. His ship put itself back together and he sailed off again. We heard laughter and him singing as he disappeared from our view. I felt a loss at seeing him leave and knowing that this was the last time we would ever see him again.

I gathered myself and tried to think of what to do next. Suddenly I was tackled to the ground and I heard a familiar voice shouting in my ear. I struggled against my attacker and managed to get hold of a leg. I bit down and laughed as I heard a roar of disapproval. All resistance disappeared and I quickly got back to my feet.

I looked over at someone who looked exactly like me, if a bit more polished. Although, his brown hair was curlier and looked in desperate need of a brush. We grinned at each other and just stared for a moment. Both of us unable to believe that this was happening.

Clay broke the silence, "What are you doing here?" He laughed, but then immediately concern broke across his face and he rushed towards me. He spoke urgently, "How did you get here? You shouldn't be here, Lino!"

I happily pushed him backwards, "I came to bring you home, you great oaf. Why would you just disappear on us like that?" I laughed, "You could've at least told me you were trying to catch the last leaf. We're partners, we do everything together."

"Catch the last leaf. What are you talking about? Are you talking about that old fairy tale that uncle Telly would tell us?"

I laughed at the confusion on his face, I was so happy to see him, and I had missed all his jokes. I had quickly learnt that being naïve around Clay was dangerous, and now I was always on the watch for his pranks. This was an odd one, but I still would not let him catch me out.

Out of the corner of my eye I saw Leah and quickly said, "Of course, so sorry. Clay, Leah is here as well. She came with me when I caught the last leaf. Quite a sneaky move on her part, but I'm glad she did. I'm not sure if I would've made it this far without her." I frowned at the look on Leah's face. She was holding her stomach and looked as if she were about to be sick. I figured the shock of seeing Clay after thinking we would never find him must be getting to her.

Clay smiled tightly and said, "Leah, it's good to see you. Although I would've preferred different circumstances."

Leah just nodded and looked away; I saw the beginning of tears in her eyes. I remembered my jealousy at thinking she had had come because she liked Clay. My confidence faltered, but I quickly distracted myself by focusing back on Clay, "You need to tell me everything."

This seemed to bring Clay out of his slum and his eyes sparkled with mischief. He always loved being able to tell a splendid adventure story, especially when he was involved. He said, "Let me show you around while I tell you."

He began walking towards a road that glittered golden. For the first time, I realised that every road seemed coated in gold. I looked at the men at the docks and froze. They were at least eight feet tall and were all well-muscled. The thing that stopped me in my tracks was that they seemed other worldly. A power radiated from them and their faces faintly shone.

Their presence reminded me of the main shining building, and it seemed as if these men were mini beacons reflecting the same light. I knew that I had no desire to get on their nasty side, each one looked like they could dispose of me without breaking a sweat. Clay called, and I quickly headed after him.

"That's not normal, right? Did you see those guys, who are they?"

"I think they're called gardiens, but it's difficult to get anyone to properly talk to you in this place." Frustration entered Clay's voice, "They keep saying I need to talk to the Prince first. I understand that I need to, but I want to explore more before…" His voice trailed off, and he seemed lost in his own thoughts.

I asked, "Is that why it's taken you so long to get here? I don't blame you for not going to the Prince, I've had a bad feeling about him since the beginning."

Clay nodded slowly, "I guess so. I also got trapped in a lot of the lies that everyone was selling me. I think I fell for every person's story and promises of glory. I guess it would've helped if I had you there with me, you were always the smart one. I should've listened to you more."

Clay's confession surprised me, I had always felt like I was the slow one when we were together, struggling to grasp a lot of what he said. His plans always seemed sophisticated, and he spoke with such confidence, I had never questioned him. His tone was bothering me, like he had given up, I tried to lighten his mood, "I had Leah with me, without her I wouldn't have left the first place."

I looked at Leah and smiled, but she was still avoiding looking at us. I asked, "So how did you get here? What happened to you?"

Clay continued speaking as if he hadn't heard me, "You've changed, you're more sure of yourself, more grown-up." A look of respect had entered his eyes as he watched me, but he quickly broke his gaze and looked around us at the changing scenery.

The large buildings around us were fading away into long green plains. Well-trimmed hedges and water fountains were scattered on the grass with arching canopies and small picnic tables. I looked behind us, the buildings seemed unnaturally far away.

There's no way we could've walked through all those large houses so quickly, and now we seemed impossibly far away from them in as few steps. All of this was too weird, and with Clay and Leah acting strange, it was time to get out of here.

Clay was still distractedly talking, "I'm actually glad you found me, this whole experience has been so strange, I never thought I would ever see anyone I knew again. I've learnt some hard lessons along my journey. It feels as if this whole place was designed to reveal all my shortcomings." He sighed.

I'd never seen him look so beaten down before, I realised with a start that he even looked skinnier than usual. Clay looked at me with sad eyes, "I'm so sorry for everything I did to you. I wasn't a good big brother; I should've been better." Clay pulled out an envelope and ran his thumb across the wax seal. He sighed and put it back in his pocket.

I didn't like this at all, Clay acting like this had put a heavy ball in my stomach. Leah was still looking worried, and now we were already on one of the bridges leading to the middle island. Everything felt like it was happening too quickly, like we were being rushed to finish the journey. I stopped as I heard voices float towards us, the sound was clear and sweet, yet also filled with strength. A determined look entered Clay's eyes and he took a step towards the voices.

I caught his arm, "Let's go. I'm sure if we go back to where we started, there must be some way to get home. This doesn't feel right. Please let's go."

Clay smiled a sad smile, and he gave me a hug, "I'm so proud of you." We broke apart and he took a deep breath, "Everything will be fine. Trust me." His old confident look returned, and he continued walking.

Leah took my hand and gave it a squeeze, "Come on."

Again, the journey seemed too short and we were suddenly standing beside one of the large pillars. I ran my hand along its smooth surface. The sound of footsteps pulled my attention. A white-haired man with a flowing robe walked towards us. He held a clipboard and carried himself with a dignified air.

He smiled and bowed his head to us, "Welcome, Clay. Happy to see you, may I have your letter please?"

Clay's hands shook as he retrieved the envelope and handed it to the man. The man saw us for the first time and gave a small start. He looked down at his list and then back at us, "You're not on the list."

Clay let out a sigh of relief, and said, "No, they're not. They followed me here."

The man frowned and looked from his list to us. His muttering to himself told me that this was a not common occurrence, and he looked lost for a moment. He seemed to make up his mind, "Wait here. I'll be back." Without another word he turned and scuffled away.

Leah watched the man leave with a worried frown, but Clay seemed to have relaxed and had turned to look the way we had come. I wondered what would happen if the man turned us away, what if we weren't allowed to see the Prince. The nervous ball in my stomach had grown and I found myself pacing to calm down. The music still floated through the air.

I looked where the man had gone and tried to make him appear by force of will. Despite the large space, there were many walls and angles that hid your view from what was further in. It didn't come across as a place that one could easily navigate. You'd probably get lost and never get to the Prince, I wondered if that was purposeful. Only those with a guide would be able to meet the Prince, anyone who tried to sneak in would become lost and most likely be caught.

The man appeared and quickly headed towards us. He smiled and bowed again, "Welcome, Lino. Welcome, Leah. The Prince welcomes you to his home. All of you, please follow me. The Prince is ready to see you."

Clay held his head high and followed the man. Leah and I hesitated a moment before following. We had come this far, there's no turning back now. I could feel myself shaking. We took a corner and came into a long hallway; a white carpet covered the stone floor. The walls were filled with colour, I looked closer and realised that the walls were covered in faces.

Millions of faces were painted onto the walls and they all smiled as if they had been given their favourite present. But the paintings were so realistic that their smiles looked genuine and warmed the hallway. I tried to keep my eyes locked on the path ahead, but out of the corner of my eye, the walls began to shift and move.

My eyes snapped back to the walls and I froze as I watched the faces change into scenes of people's lives. Birthdays, first days of school, graduations, marriages, the key moments of people's lives played out. Before I knew what I was doing, I had taken steps toward the moving images. I asked, "What is this?"

The man answered quietly as if not to disturb the lives around us, "The Prince loves to know what his people are up to, it's his greatest joy to be part of their lives."

I watched as a young boy sat in his room, alone, and crying. Anger flooded me and I said, "If he loves his people so much, why would he let this happen?" I knew my anger was misplaced, but I was tired of hearing of this Prince's greatness, when I had never seen any evidence of it, "There's no point of power, if he can't do anything with it."

The man's eyes filled with sympathy, but his gaze was steady, "You can ask him yourself."

I became aware of the singing again, this time it sounded as if there was a choir in the walls. Unable to look at the wall any longer, I turned away and readied myself for what was to come. My anger burned inside me, and I felt as if it would consume me. I didn't fully understand where it came from, and why it was directed at the Prince, but my anger was focused against him.

The man with the clip board stopped before a large wooden door. The door was at least two stories tall and looked of impenetrable strength. I wondered how it was going to open. Our guide said, "Are you ready?"

We looked at each other and nodded.

All of a sudden, a crack appeared, and light streamed through the small opening. The singing exploded all around us and I took a step back. I felt light-headed and my legs wobbled from the power of the voices. Light enveloped us as the doors opened completely, a light touch on my back pushed me forward, and I stumbled forward. Immediately, I fell to my knees as I was overwhelmed by the presence in the room. I felt myself shaking, but realised it was out of awe, not fear.

A door at the back of the room opened and I didn't think it was possible, but even more light spilled in. As soon as the outline of a man walked into the room, I fell face down on the floor and lay shivering on the ground. It felt as if my heart were trying to explode out my chest and I felt tears streaming down my face.

I knew I was in the presence of such power as I never knew existed. A word from this man could destroy the universe. I knew it with certainty, and I feared that this was the end. His presence alone would destroy us.

Before I knew what was happening, I heard a deep rumbling voice next to me. The voice cut through the singing like it wasn't there, it was a mixture of strength and yet such tenderness that I immediately desired to hear it for the rest of my life. Nothing would make me happier than to lie here and hear the man speak for the remainder of my life.

A soft hand on my shoulder brought my head up, and I looked into the face of the Prince. His eyes were pools of warmth and small wrinkles around his eyes showed his ready smile.

He helped me to my feet and wrapped me in a tight hug. He said, "You don't know how I've longed to hug you in person." He took my head in his hands and kissed each of my cheeks, "Welcome, Lino."

I felt a sense of loss as he let go and moved to Leah. She still lay face-down on the floor, and she shook as he touched her shoulder. I found I couldn't keep my eyes off the Prince, his movements were graceful and yet powerful. Tears streamed down Leah's face as the Prince hugged her and kissed her on either cheek. Her eyes were filled with wonder and she wore a goofy grin as he spoke to her.

The Prince took a few steps back and spread his arms like a proud father showing off his children. I realised that I could see around us now, the light had either dimmed or we had gotten used to it, either way I could still feel the pulse of power in the room.

The room was bare except for paintings on the wall which depicted more faces I didn't recognize. My mouth fell open as I looked up and saw a balcony filled with white robed… things… I had no other word for them, they had human features but there was no mistaking that they were different. Strong faces, male and female, surrounded them and I was shocked to find that the music was coming from them.

The Prince talking brought me back. I listened eagerly, convinced that everything he said would be important. He was looking at Clay while he spoke, "It's been a long and difficult journey. Life is difficult and unpredictable, but you're here with me now. All pain and sorrow will cease to exist."

My heart started thumping and I struggled to focus on what was being said. This didn't seem right, why was he saying these things? I looked at Clay's face, and gratitude filled his eyes, he was nodding eagerly at the Prince's every word.

"Your journey has taught you a lot and it warms my heart that you continued through the trials to me. Well done, good and faithful son, you were faithful with your life, now you may enter into my joy."

"No!" I screamed as I realised what was happening. Leah was silently sobbing next to me. I looked from the Prince to Clay, "Please don't listen to him. You're coming home with me." I turned to the Prince, his soft kind eyes watched me, I swallowed but forced myself to speak, "You can't take him. He's my brother, I need him with me."

Clay spoke up, "Lino, this is what I'm here for. I've come to stay with the Prince."

Tears filled my eyes, but it was from anger, "No! I don't accept it." I pleaded with the Prince, "Surely you'll let him come back with me. You wouldn't have let me come here and chase after him if I couldn't get him back. I caught up to him. Surely that means something?"

Clay spoke softly, "Lino…"

"No!" I hoped if I shouted it often enough, it would become true. "You're not going anywhere without me. Please don't do this."

The sadness in the Prince's eyes softened my anger, but I refused to admit defeat. He spoke, "Lino, your journey here was for your benefit, not to rescue your brother. You needed the time to process what had happened and…"

I broke in, "But Leah's here as well. Surely, that means things can change. From the beginning, I knew that if I found Clay, then he would come back with me."

The Prince continued to speak gently, his voice was full of sympathy, "Leah being here is between her and myself. As for you, you were struggling to accept the loss of your brother. Clay begged me to help you, even if it meant a delay in his coming home to me. Each obstacle you faced has helped you come to a place where you can finally say goodbye."

Thoughts of my journey flashed through my mind, how at each place I had to overcome some emotional block and how I had learnt so much about myself through it. I remembered my time in the lake, when the cloud had hovered over a group of my memories, seeming to block their true story. The voice of my mom crying over Clay and my parents not knowing how to cope with his disappearance.

Suddenly the veil I had been covering the truth dropped off. I remembered hearing my parents receive the call that Clay had died in a car accident. They spoke in the kitchen, trying to decide how to tell me, but they hadn't known I was listening the whole time. My uncle Telly, the pastor, coming to encourage us and share comforting stories. I had pretended none of it had happened and became obsessed with finding Clay, bringing him back.

The memories overwhelmed me. My voice broke, "I can't. It's too painful." The dark cloud of memories suddenly broke, and I felt consumed by grief. A heartache filled my chest, a pain so deep, it numbed my whole body. I clamped my eyes shut and felt the water rising around my mind again, drowning me from inside. The headaches I always had came back and threatened to split my skull. I cried out and fell to my knees.

The Prince said, "Lino."

Suddenly the cloud ran out of rain and began to dissipate, a loud crack sounded, and all the water rushed out. I opened my eyes and looked at the man who had freed me, the same man who had previously drained the water. Leah gasped as if she had realised the same thing.

The pain slowly began to lessen, and my headache cleared. I sat back on my heels. I kept my eyes on the Prince and soaked up his comfort, I tried to believe that

I could trust him with anything. Even the life of my brother.

I asked, "Will I ever see him again?"

The Prince shook his head, "Not until you visit me again. For now, your brother will stay with me and you will go back home. I have big plans for you." His smile spoke of the confidence he had in me.

I took a shaky breath and looked at Clay. I couldn't bring myself to say goodbye, but Clay smiled and hugged me tightly, "It's okay to be happy again, nothing will make me happier than seeing you enjoy your life. I will be watching and cheering you on every step of the way. I love you so much, Lino! You're the best brother I could've ever asked for."

I watched as Clay got to his feet and turned to the Prince. The Prince smiled and indicated the door he had come through. The door swung open and the music increased to full volume again, this time it sounded like a celebration. A welcoming home.

Clay looked at me one last time and I could see the absolute excitement and peace in his eyes. I whispered, "I love you too. Goodbye, Clay." He walked into the light and the singing. A roar of welcoming sounded as the door closed behind him.

Home

I stared numbly at the door. I had just gotten my brother back and now he was gone. Forever. I was a mixture of feelings, unable to process what had just happened. Despite everything, I was surprised to find that I was no longer angry, I was sad - the anger had disappeared. A hollowness was inside me and I wondered if it would ever go away.

Clay not being around would be strange and I would miss him terribly, but at least I got to see him one last time, even if it was brief. It was more than I could've expected. Wherever he went, it was a place that he would be happy in, and that brought me a lot of comfort.

I imagined what life would be like without him and it scared me. It would require me to stand on my own two feet and face the world alone. Am I enough? Did I have what it takes? Despite my uncertainties, I knew that I would at least try, I would become the man that I wanted to be. No more hiding, no more letting the world pass me by.

I broke my gaze from the door and swallowed at the finality of the action. It was time to face life again and stop living in a fantasy world. I wondered how my parents were doing, and I was ashamed to realise that I was only considering their feelings now. Were they worried about me too? How long had I been gone? I needed to get back home.

The Prince and Leah were talking. It felt like a private conversation, so I kept my distance. Despite my intention, I still overheard parts of their talk. Leah asked about her mom and thanked the Prince for taking care of her. She laughed through her tears and asked many questions, as if she had been longing for this conversation for a long time. She nodded eagerly and drank up every response.

They embraced and I heard the Prince speak words of love and encouragement over her. She seemed to glow brighter with every word. Leah nodded at something the Prince said and then headed towards me.

A skip was in her step, but she slowed as she saw the look in my eyes. She lowered her eyes in embarrassment as she was reminded of what had just happened. She said, "Sorry Lino, I shouldn't have..."

"It's fine, Leah, I'm doing okay. I guess I had known Clay was gone, but I didn't want to face it." I studied her face and asked the question that had been eating at me, "Did you know the whole time?"

Leah shook her head, "Now I remember your mom coming to tell us, but when we got here it seemed to have been wiped from my memory. Along the way, I began suspecting it, but I only remembered as we arrived in the city. I'm so sorry, Lino." She buried her face in my chest.

I put my arms around her and enjoyed the comfort she brought. I began to feel the emptiness begin to fill. A light cough from the Prince brought us back. Leah smiled up at me and said, "The Prince is sending me back home. He wants to talk to you, and then you'll come too?" She ended it as a question and a look of worry passed over her face.

I nodded, "I'll see you soon."

Leah let out a breath in relief and smiled. She gave me a kiss on the cheek and as she walked back to the Prince, she shimmered and was gone. I blinked in surprise. The Prince looked at me and smiled. I asked, "Did she go home?"

He nodded and said, "It's not her time either."

I found I couldn't look into his eyes. I didn't know what to say to him, and I was still unsure what I thought about him. I understood that it was Clay's time to go, but I still felt it was unfair, and that the Prince could've done something to make it different. I felt the bubble of anger rise again. I needed some way to let out how I was feeling, and I was still reeling from what was happening. My emotions felt numb, but at the same time sharpened and on edge. I blinked away the tears that began to form and focused on my feet. The sight of the sandals brought a squawked laugh, "These are so impractical. I hate wearing them."

Still avoiding his eyes, I looked over at the Prince, and watched him wiggle his toes in his sandals. It was such an odd sight that it brought another fit of laughter. The Prince seemed to be holding back laughter as well, he said, "I've gotten used to them, I never imagined that everyone would copy me. I fear I've started the worst fashion trend imaginable."

A crazed laugh overtook me, I feared that I'd suddenly gone mad. I tried to speak between wheezes of laughter and taking breaths, "I wrestled a giant, spoke to an eagle, walked through mountains, forests and the desert while wearing sandals."

I struggled to breathe, "I did it all to find Clay, and now he's gone." My laughter died as suddenly as it had started. I breathed deeply. I looked at what had carried me through my journey, and I was filled with fury. I ripped them off and threw the sandals across the room. I screamed in anger. I whirled around and looked the Prince in the eyes. His gaze stopped me immediately.

My last wall of resistance disappeared as I looked into those eyes. Those kind, beautiful eyes. Wisdom and power beyond measure floated in his gaze, yet he was giving me his full attention. No anger, no judgement, only a calm sadness that echoed how I was feeling. The pain in his eyes broke me. I fell to my knees and cried, "Why did he have to go? I can't…" My sobs stopped me from talking.

A fresh wave of pain flowed through me, it was so strong I felt like crawling into a ball and disappearing. My tears continued to flow as I mourned the loss of my big brother. All the time we had spent together and laughed at things only we found funny. Our arguments and fights, but always ending up on the same team in the end. I would be all alone now. The emptiness inside me cried out. I felt that I was going to be swallowed and never return.

I whispered, "Please help me." I looked up and was shocked to see tears on the Prince's cheeks. He held his arms open, and I immediately stumbled back to my feet and ran towards him. I knew there was safety in his arms, and it was the only thing that would help me heal. I fell into his embrace and continued crying.

He spoke softly, "It pains me to see my people hurting. The time is coming when all that will come to an end, but for now we need to stick together, and I'll help you through it."

It began slowly, but my thoughts quietened, and I relaxed into his arms. The same peace that I experienced in the lake came back, and I realised that this man was the source of the water. Nothing else could ever satisfy me as much as his presence could. The aching hollowness inside me began to fill as I clung to the Prince. The pain was still there, but now I felt like it wouldn't consume me entirely.

I said, "What am I going to do without him? He's always been around and now I will be alone. Life is going to be so empty." I took another deep breath and sighed.

A tightness in my chest loosened. More peace flowed into me, and slowly I began to accept what had happened. It was going to be hard without Clay around, but I still had a family back home, and Leah. I would miss Clay terribly, but I needed to continue living. It's what he had wanted.

The Prince took my head in his hands, "Remember me, and live your life with me in your heart. I will guide you and be there every step of the way. The journey won't be easy, but I'll be with you. I have big plans for you." He kissed me on the forehead and my world darkened.

Branches swayed above my eyes and I watched the green leaves rippling in the breeze. I lay on my back and enjoyed the warmth from the sun on my skin. A leaf broke free and fell towards me, I caught it and stared in wonder.

Everything came back to me in a rush and I leapt to my feet. I turned around and saw my house, same as it's always been, but it was beautiful to me. I looked to the tree next to me and saw its bare branches, not a single leaf left. I took a deep breath, Clay was in a better place, a place where he would always be happy, and nothing could ever hurt him again.

I wondered at how my tree had recovered all its leaves. It looked full of life and I smiled as I felt the same thing. Clay's had the beginnings of new growth. The two other trees in the garden were looking worn and tired, but they also stood strong.

I ran back towards the house. I burst through the back door and called out. At first there was silence, but then shouts came from upstairs. I smiled broadly as my parents rushed down the stairs, with uncle Telly close behind. I was shocked by how tired they looked, my mom's hair was unbrushed and my dad had dark lines under his eyes. They paused at the bottom of the stairs as if to make sure I was really there.

"Hi." I said sheepishly.

They yelled with happiness and rushed towards me, wrapping me in hugs and kisses. Uncle Telly laughed and slapped me on the back. My mom took my head in her hands and stared at me. She had tears in her eyes and continued to kiss me everywhere. I laughed and disentangled myself from the onslaught of affection. My dad took my shoulder and gave it a squeeze.

Uncle Telly asked, "Where've you been? You just disappeared."

I grew sombre for the first time and looked at my parents, "Sorry for disappearing on you. I would like to say it's not my fault, but it was something I desperately needed."

I took a deep breath and launched into the story, "It started with me catching the last leaf…" Their eyes grew larger with each word, but uncle Telly beamed with happiness.

As I told them about finding Clay and then meeting the Prince, their eyes filled with tears. My voice broke as I continued speaking, but I smiled throughout. My parents had an arm around each other, and my mom had a hand over her mouth. She clapped happily as I told her that Clay had looked as happy as I'd ever seen him and what had awaited him through the door.

"So, you met the Prince?" Uncle Telly asked with a knowing look in his eyes.

I nodded, "He's everything a Prince should be, and nothing like I'd expected. He was the most amazing person I'd ever met, and I will never forget the look in his eyes. Those eyes would melt the hardest heart and bring anyone to their knees. There's no one I'd rather trust Clay with than that man."

I looked at my parents again, "I'm sorry for disappearing on you. I know this time hasn't been easy for you and I just made it harder, but when I found out that Clay had died, I hadn't known what to do. I felt like part of me had died with him. I remembered the stories about the last leaf, and I became obsessed. I refused to admit what had happened and convinced myself that if I could only see him again, then I could bring him back."

My mom spoke, "It's okay, we understand. It was difficult seeing you go through so much pain and not being able to do anything to help. We were worried you would do something to yourself."

Dad spoke, "I'm amazed so much happened, you were only gone here for two days, but it sounded like you spend a couple of weeks on your journey. But I'm glad you're back."

"So am I. I missed you all so much." We hugged, and I smiled at how lucky I was to have a family that loved me so much. And a Prince that watched over all of us.

I knocked on Leah's door, practically bouncing on my feet. She opened the door and smiled broadly as she saw me. Behind her I saw her dad and stepmom wiping teary faces. They smiled happily, but my eyes were only for Leah. She looked beautiful in a dark green dress and her eyes were dark pools that pulled me in.

We stepped towards each other and embraced. Happiness burst inside me and I couldn't help but laugh. I remembered the Prince's last words telling me that he had great plans for me, and as I held Leah, I realised I couldn't wait for what was to come.

Devon Hoole

Epilogue: Grief

Grief is something that everyone must deal with at some point in their life. The loss comes in different forms, but the feelings are the same. It is difficult to understand and make sense of the depth of pain that can be experienced while grieving. The hollowness, yet at the same time, an overflow of emotion that threatens to consume you. For most, a scar remains forever. Always aching as your thoughts wander. It's a journey that many go on and we often find ourselves getting lost in the process. How can something so common be so misunderstood?

There's no right way to grieve, and it is often a journey we choose to take alone. We want to be heroes and take on the pain ourselves. Not wanting to be a burden to others. Despite our loved ones trying to comfort us, no one can replace the one who was lost. We know that they mean well, but lives will continue and soon it will only be a faint memory. How long should the lost one be mourned for? Is it all right to continue my own life? Why do I feel guilty when I take pleasure in life again and realise that I'm beginning to forget?

What am I doing with my own life? Is success what I desire? Will it be enough? Life gains a different perspective during grief. The big things can lose meaning and the small acts become important, like loving those around you and being content with what you have.

The Last Leaf

An important question arises as to what happens to people after they die. What's next? Do they cease to exist, or reincarnate as something new, or is there life after death? Your beliefs can be challenged during this time, and it will lead you on another journey of discovery. Some come out the other side with renewed faith, while others have abandoned any previous beliefs. When their time comes, they will figure it out for themselves.

If you are struggling with grief and miss your loved one. Take your pain to Jesus and hand it over to Him. He is the One who can heal your aching heart. He is the One who will be there for you when it feels like no one else is. It's not easy and can be scary to let go, but know that God is trustworthy and will take care of your loved one.

As for me, I know that there is a God who will welcome me into His arms when my time comes. Until then, I know that He has always been with me and I am honoured to live my life on Earth for Him.

Devon Hoole

ABOUT THE AUTHOR

Devon Hoole is twenty-four years old and lives in Cape Town, South Africa. He is a Registered Counsellor as well as currently completing his Master's Degree in Community Mental Health Promotion. He is also the author of *Delivered* and *Forgiven*. Currently he is working on his new book *Exodus*.